AN UNTIDY END

BLYTHE BAKER

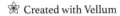

Anna Fairweather stands on the brink of discovering the answers to questions that have haunted her since childhood. Still, danger looms over her...

When Anna, Jerome, and Mrs. Montford journey from London to Venice in search of a missing person, a train conductor turns up dead. Can Anna capture the murderer before they reach their destination?

1

I had never been so nervous for a meeting in all my life.

"Now, you will be just fine, dear," said Sister Agnes, straightening a stack of books on the low table in the middle of the parlor. "I hear that he is a generous man, with a wonderful reputation here in London. Nothing but good things, I assure you."

I nodded, not trusting my words as I straightened my hair in the small round mirror that hung near the window. I wished I had not cut it so short. I was already beginning to miss my long hair and the means of keeping it up out of my face.

"Goodness, this room is a mess," Sister Agnes said, fluttering around like a bird searching for twigs for her nest. "This is what happens when there has not been a family here for nearly a month!"

I glanced over my shoulder at the tufted settee, remembering the last time the room had been used for me. I could not have been older than seven or eight. A couple far too old for children of their own had come, searching for some young life to bring into their home.

I had every hope that they might adopt me...until we received a letter from the husband nearly a fortnight after our meeting, explaining that the wife and her sister had been killed in a tragic car accident just outside the city.

"Oh, it is *exciting,* though, is it not?" Sister Agnes said, beaming as she straightened to look at me. "I realize this might not be the precise outcome you had hoped for but an *opportunity* it most certainly is! To be taken into the home of a Colonel! My dear, you are most fortunate."

"Yes, I am," I said. "And so soon after turning eighteen."

"Indeed, dear. It seems as if this was your destiny all along," Sister Agnes said, smoothing her skirts.

A knock from the door out in the foyer sent my heart racing in nervous palpitations.

Sister Agnes regarded me with large blue eyes. "Oh, that must be him now!" she exclaimed. "Allow me to fetch him. You stay right there. And smile, girl, smile! You are so lovely when you allow yourself to smile once in a while!"

She scurried from the room like an excited squirrel.

I let out a breath that had caught in my chest.

This is it...the moment I have been both looking forward to and dreading all week.

"Good afternoon, sir, good afternoon," Sister Agnes said brightly. "Please, please, come in. We are positively *honored* to have you."

"Thank you very much, Sister," the man said. "It is my pleasure to be here."

Footsteps sounded in the hall, followed quickly by the distinct *cli-click* of the door closing.

"I trust you are well, sir?"

"Very well, thank you," he said. "I had no idea that this charming place was tucked away in this part of town. As charming as an orphanage can be, of course."

"Oh, yes, we are very blessed here," Sister Agnes said, not at all displeased by his words. "Our children are happy, healthy, and the majority find homes within a year or two of coming into our care."

"That is wonderful news," the man said. It sounded as if he meant it.

"Right through here, Colonel. She is waiting for you!" Sister Agnes said.

I heard her frantic steps scurry away down the hall and the heavier set of steps stop just outside in the hall.

The city of London stretched out before me. In the distance, I could see the smoke billowing from the towering brick stacks from the cannery. The bells from the church on the corner began to chime noon, filling the air with their melodic hymn. Cars passed by on the street, engines rumbling and wheels crunching on the cobblestone.

It mattered little what I saw, however. I might have seen a three-headed dog pass by and I knew it would have done little to ease my frantic heart.

"Ah...Anna Fairweather, I presume?"

I turned from my place at the window, my hands clenched before me. "Yes?"

The kindly man who stood in the doorway removed his hat. "My name is Colonel Montford. Might I have a word?"

He was taller than I had expected, with a wide frame and muscular stature that certainly demonstrated the years of hard work and physical exertion that came from serving in the military. His sandy hair, going grey around his ears, had been trimmed close to his head in a fashion I imagined he had not changed in many years.

"Of course, Colonel. Please come in and have a seat," I said, gesturing to one of the empty chairs across from the settee.

"Thank you," he said, and did so.

He peered up at me, letting his hat rest upon his knees.

"I presume that Sister...Margaret, yes? Sister Margaret explained to you my reason for coming to speak with you today?" he asked.

"Yes, sir," I said, taking a seat on the settee across from him. I made sure to sit as straight as I could, keeping all of my lessons of how to behave like a lady at the forefront of my mind. I folded my hands in my lap and kept my expression neutral. *"It does not do for a lady to slouch, nor to smile too freely, lest she is seen as a fool and a ne'er-do-well."* "She shared with me the letter that you so kindly sent. You are hoping to find a young lady to provide care and support for your wife. Is that correct?"

"Yes, in a matter of speaking," he said, buttoning up the front of his coat. "Though I suppose that does all sound a bit formal, doesn't it? That is not at all how I wanted it to seem..."

I wondered why he would say it that way. Was he not hiring me for a position in his home? It should be the very definition of formality.

"What I mean by that is that we are hiring you as a maid on my household staff, yes, but your position is special. My wife is very dear to me, as you can imagine, and I wish to ensure that she has someone with her at all times. You will help her get ready in the mornings and stay with her if she needs anything during her meals. I hope she can find some comfort in having you nearby, knowing she can rely upon you to help her."

He gave me a smile but it seemed...heavy. Sad.

"She and I are both getting on in our years and we do not have the energy that we once did. I know that she would be rather cross with me for saying so but she would certainly benefit from having someone there to give her support. The only reason I have been able to convince her is because..."

His voice trailed off and he gave me a brief but pointed look.

He chuckled.

"My apologies. I suppose there are matters that I should remain discreet about."

He clapped his hands together.

"Is this arrangement still agreeable to you? Have I managed to clarify it further?"

"Oh, yes, sir," I said with a firm nod. "It is most agreeable."

"And you are all packed? Ready to go?" he asked, looking around behind him for what I could only assume were my belongings.

"Yes, sir," I said. "Everything is gathered up in the hall."

"Brilliant," he said, slapping his knees before standing up once more. "Then we should not delay."

He strode toward the doorway, pausing only for a moment to glance at me over his shoulder.

"Of course, you may take some time to say goodbye to whomever you wish," he said. "I realize this has been your home for many years now, and while you may be ready to be off on your next adventure, it does not mean that leaving will not prove difficult."

"I...thank you, Colonel. That would be...that would be wonderful."

The goodbyes came with more tears than I might have expected.

The younger children did not seem to fully understand that I would be leaving for good and that I was not being adopted by the Colonel, only given a post in his home. The idea seemed entirely foreign to them, as they waited for a family of their own to come and whisk them away to a better life. In a way, it made me regret that I had not found a family, but as I could remember my own father with some clarity, I did not think I ever would have been able to fully embrace them as my true parents.

It was better this way, I told the children. And in my heart, I knew it to be true.

I shared boisterous goodbyes with some of the girls I had shared a room with for many years. Isabelle, with the singing voice that would one day rival the greatest in opera; Nancy, with a vocabulary as extensive as the library we would visit every second Saturday; Olivia, with a wit and charm sure to win the hearts of any family.

I would miss them. They and the Sisters who had made it their life's work to care for the other children and I.

"I owe you everything," I told Sister Agnes and Sister Mary as the Colonel's driver carried my trunk out to the car, only half filled with all of the possessions I had to my name. It was a meager collection, some of which had been gifted from the other children.

"You are a good girl," Sister Mary said with a pat against my cheek. I could see her green eyes shining with unshed tears behind her round spectacles.

"Yes, dear, and you will do very well," Sister Agnes added. "I assure you, this is where you are *meant* to be. I know it."

She squeezed my hands in her own. "Now, do not forget to write to us," she said.

"Yes, the children will love to know how you are," Sister Mary agreed. "This might be a new chapter but that does not mean that you need to fear it."

"Yes, yes," Sister Agnes said, beaming.

I stared through the window at the front door of the place that had been my home for twelve years but that would be no longer. My home for the foreseeable future was a place that I had not yet laid eyes upon.

"There, now," the Colonel said awkwardly to me as we pulled away from the curb, the hum of the car dulling the ringing in my ears. "Do not despair. I think you will find our home in Maidstone to be pleasant. Quite pleasant, indeed."

I turned to look at him and saw that he was staring intently at me.

My face colored and I opened my mouth to speak. Perhaps there was something on my face?

"Oh, do forgive me..." he said with a nervous chuckle. "You bear a striking resemblance to someone I...to someone I once knew."

"Well, sir, I do hope that association is not an unpleasant one," I said, suddenly uneasy.

"Not at all," the Colonel said. "In fact, this person...well, he was a dear friend of mine."

His eyes became suddenly distant.

"I rather miss him, if I may be so honest."

"I am sorry for your loss," I said.

He looked for a moment as if he might say more but instead turned to stare out the window at the rows of houses passing us by.

We arrived at the train station less than half an hour later. While aboard, the Colonel told me what my duties and my new life would be like. He certainly seemed to have enough energy to speak for the both of us, which I was all too happy to allow him to do.

"Now, you will have to realize that my dear Beatrice is a bit of...well, she's a bit of a stickler," the Colonel said as we approached their estate in Maidstone later that afternoon.

"Which is why I think you will be a very good fit for her. She prefers her life to be just so, you see, and she does not take kindly to anything being out of sorts. Her schedule, her plans, anything."

"She will not have to worry with me at all, sir," I said. "I was known for being a bit strict at the orphanage. It rather displeased some of the more spirited children when I would try to whip them into shape."

He nodded approvingly. "Good. You and she will get along swimmingly."   ·

Mrs. Montford had a stern expression to match the desire for her life to be "just so" when I met her. A great deal more reserved than her exuberant husband, she gave me a small, practiced smile at our introduction and nothing more.

"You know how to do laundry?" Mrs. Montford asked, her steely blue eyes sharper than even Sister Margaret's.

"Yes, ma'am," I said, my hands clutched together in front of me, my only form of support.

"And cooking and cleaning?" she asked.

"Yes, ma'am," I said. "I have experience in them all."

She gave me a nod. "Good. What of horses? What do you know of them?"

"I must confess that I do not have a great deal of experience with horses," I admitted in a low voice, averting my gaze. My face turned scarlet. *Did Sister Margaret know that this might be one of the requirements?*

"Come now, my dear, she can learn to manage your riding things," the Colonel said with a boisterous laugh. "She is a very good fit, don't you think?"

"I suppose she will do," Mrs. Montford said.

She gave me a scrutinizing gaze, her eyes flashing.

It is going to be some time before she trusts me, I realized. *I wonder why she seems so guarded?*

"Very good," Colonel Montford said. "I have had Mr. Hendrick set you up in the empty room at the end of the hall, Anna. I realize that you will not be sleeping where most of the staff sleeps, but I thought it better for you to be close to Mrs. Montford, as she is your primary concern." He smiled. "Well, now, why don't you go on down there and get yourself unpacked? We shall have the housekeeper, Mrs. Carlisle, give you a full tour in the morning. For now, get some rest and something to eat down in the kitchen, whenever you feel so inclined. I shall have you report in the parlor at seven sharp to begin your day."

"Of course, sir," I said, dipping into a curtsy. "It was an honor to meet you, Mrs. Montford. I look forward to having the chance to serve you."

Mrs. Montford's expression hardened and she looked down. "Off you go, girl," she said, a slightly coolness in her tone.

"Yes, ma'am. Of course."

I stepped out of the room and looked up and down the hall both ways.

Which way is my room?

I hesitated just out of sight for a moment, debating whether or not I should go back and ask where, precisely, I was to be staying, when I heard my name.

"Anna, you said?" she asked. "I can hardly dare to believe it... I never would have imagined – "

"I know, my dear, I know," the Colonel said, his voice heavy with conviction. "Looks just like him, doesn't she?"

"It's uncanny, really..." Mrs. Montford replied. "And you – "

"Not a word," he said. "She would not understand anyway, would she?"

"No, I suppose not," Mrs. Montford said. "Still..."

"I know..." he said. "I wish it had all turned out differently, too..."

I knew my opportunity to ask for directions had passed. If I returned, they would know I had been eavesdropping.

I started down the hall as quietly as I could, my heart heavy.

Whoever this man is that I remind them of so much, he must have meant a great deal to them.

Was it a child? A brother? A cousin? Or perhaps nothing more than a friend, just as the Colonel had said

Regardless, I knew it was none of my business. The Colonel had assured me that I reminded him of good things. From that, I could take comfort.

I certainly hoped it would not affect Mrs. Montford's impression of me.

Perhaps that is why she was so cold upon our greeting, I thought. *Perhaps looking at me was far too much of a shock.*

I consoled myself with these thoughts as I peered into the last room at the end of the hall and discovered my trunk sitting at the end of the small bed.

Leaving my worries out in the hall, I closed the door behind me and began to settle in to my new home...and my new life.

2

————

"He...what?" I breathed.

"The Colonel..." Mrs. Montford said, her voice shaky. "He...did kill your father. But only because your father asked him to."

I hadn't expected her to admit the truth. It was as if someone had suddenly sat on my chest, pressing the air from my lungs. Fog snaked into my mind, diluting all thoughts, making it impossible to remember what I had even been thinking before – before –

"This – this is all coming out wrong," Mrs. Montford said, the lines around her eyes and mouth becoming prominent. "I will explain it properly."

As I stared at her, I had a startling recollection of the first time we had met. Back then, I had been frightened of her. Now, she behaved as if it was she who ought to be frightened.

"Here... Have a seat, Anna. Just in case."

The soothing tone registered somewhere in the back of my mind and I looked around to see Jerome looking down at me with those clear, blue eyes...

He gave me a small, encouraging smile.

I did not fight him. I allowed him to gently slip his hand through the crook of my arm and help ease me down into the chair beside him.

Mrs. Montford, lips pursed and face as pale as freshly fallen snow, looked around indecisively. "Oh..." she said. "What would the Colonel say? He would be furious – or would he?"

"Aunt Bea, please..." Jerome said. "I do not mean to rush you but I believe it would be best if you were to explain all this to Anna."

Mrs. Montford looked as if she had been awoken where she stood, with wide eyes and an eerie stillness. "Yes..." she said. "Yes, of course."

She seemed to gather herself enough to walk across the room to the chair beside me and take a seat there.

"Anna..." she said. "What I am going to tell you may not make a great deal of sense to you. You see, your father was very dear to the Colonel and me."

Icy fingers closed around my heart, gripping it enough to send shivers down my spine. *They knew my father? How – how could they –*

Mrs. Montford looked down at her hands stretched out across her lap.

"I fear I have put off considering what I might do if I were ever to tell you this," she said. "I hoped that if I ever needed to, it might be in a letter I left for you after I died."

The knots tightened in my stomach. Why? Why did she want to keep this information from me? Hot anger burst through the icy splinters in my chest.

"I suppose I should start at the beginning," Mrs. Montford said. "Or at least, as far back as might be relevant to you. The Colonel met your father at a banquet for an old military general in London, some forty years ago. Your father was a young man, then, but the Colonel found him quite sharp and amusing. The two men got on well. We invited him and his lovely young wife, your mother, to our home on a number of occasions for dinner, as we enjoyed their company. As the years went on, the Colonel and I grew older, but the two men stayed close. Then something happened, around twenty-two years ago...You were born, Anna."

My heartbeats came unsteadily.

"The friendship between us all faded, about that time..." Mrs. Montford said. "Your father grew serious about his profession and tried to clean himself up for the betterment of you and your mother. He tried to leave all of his bad habits behind, habits he had made when he was young."

Seeing her face fall, I braced myself for unpleasant information.

"...So when certain old *associates* of his came looking for him some years after your mother died, he knew that he needed help."

I could do nothing more than stare at her. Questions bubbled to the surface of my mind but nothing more coherent than feelings of "Who," and "Why."

"He...owed money to dangerous people, you see," Mrs. Montford said. "From years before. He thought the matter had been resolved, but when these criminals managed to track him down, they demanded an exorbitant sum, with interest. Otherwise, they threatened to take his life in payment. He did not have that sort of money. That being the case, he feared for your life, knowing they would not stop at taking his."

My heart jumped in my chest, like a horse struck on its flanks. "I do not understand," I said. "My father was a banker. At least, that is what I remember him as. Something respectable."

"And he was," Mrs. Montford said. "But he, like many young men, had been seduced by the idea of monetary gain. He allowed himself to be lured into some unsavory business dealings on the side."

I had always thought highly of my father, perhaps even put him atop a pedestal of great honor, as a response to his death. I knew no one to be perfect but I had never seen failings in him when I was young. As such, to hear something so real and human about him hit me a great deal like having my knees swept out from underneath me.

"That is when he came to my husband," Mrs. Montford said. "It had been some time since the two had been together; your father was heartbroken after your mother died and spoke to very few people for a long time. The Colonel had been the one to talk him out of his dangerous dealings soon after your birth. He helped him square away what he needed to and used some of his connections to help extricate your father from arrangements."

"What sort of arrangements were these?" I asked. "What did my father really do?"

Mrs. Montford's expression softened. "It was nothing as terrible as you might be thinking, dear," she said. "He helped thieves pawn off valuable items. It was additional income for him and his professional position was such that no one would suspect him of it."

Nausea cut through some of the fear and anger, mingling with great disappointment.

"The men who came looking for him...well, it seemed that your father had not given them the full worth of an item they had sold him some years before. When they learned of its true value, they came looking for him for the remaining amount. From what the Colonel told me, the item was a ring from an old and noble family. Your father had not previously understood its value and did not have the money to pay what they demanded." She frowned. "The Colonel told me it was an absurd sum, one that no man alone would have been able to pay. He believed that to be the point. They wanted his life, not his money, in revenge for what they saw as a slight."

I swallowed, my jaw beginning to ache as I clenched it tightly shut.

"Your father..." Mrs. Montford said. "He came to the Colonel one night, terribly late, in such a fright. He feared there was only one solution. No matter how they attempted to work out another possibility, they both continued to come to the same reality..."

She looked at me, her eyes shining.

"Either your father was killed by someone else, and you protected...or the both of you would lose your lives at the hands of those...those detestable – "

She cleared her throat, and I saw her fists clench for a brief second.

"And so, he asked the Colonel to be the one to kill him..." I asked, finding it difficult to form the words, given how tight my throat had become.

"No, no..." Mrs. Montford said, with an anxious shake of her head. "Not at all. I went about this all wrong..."

She sighed again, and I noticed a flash in her eyes.

"Your father asked the Colonel to make it *appear* as if he had been killed," Mrs. Montford said. "He wanted nothing more than to fake his death and flee the city."

"Flee...?"

"The plan was that your father should appear to be 'attacked' by an anonymous thief in the street and drowned in the river," she said. "The Colonel heartily agreed to play the role and promised that he would tell the story of witnessing the event. As I recall...that very night, he rushed to the police and told them the tale precisely as they had rehearsed it. It was for your safety, of course. It was all meant to be a means of protecting you. I assume my husband believed you would have pieced together some of the truth over the years, given what he left for you in his will."

I frowned. "His will? What do you – "

It all came rushing back. It had felt an eternity ago. Before moving to London. Before the trip to Brighton. Before everything with Jerome...

The late Colonel had left me a sizable amount, unbeknownst to everyone in the extended family who did not receive a single coin. I had not thought about it in such a long time...

For reasons known to her. That was what he had written in his will.

Was this what he had meant?

"I believe it was his way of trying to make amends to you," Mrs. Montford said.

I felt as if the entirety of my world, the very foundation of my life, had shifted. What I had always thought to be true, the very core of who I was, crumbled away beneath me.

In that moment, I did not know whether I should feel moved or disgusted by her telling me all of this.

Did the Colonel think that his money could change what had happened? Did he believe giving me a position in his home and leaving me a modest inheritance would somehow make what he had kept from me right?

I slowly turned my eyes up to Mrs. Montford.

"You knew? You knew all this time..." I murmured.

She nodded. "It has been very difficult all these years to say nothing to you about it."

3

———

"Why?" I asked, anger consuming all thought. "Why did you keep this from me? After all this time, after all these years..."

"You have every right – every reason – to be upset," Mrs. Montford said. "But you must understand, it was his wish. Your father's wish."

"Why?" I asked again. I wondered how many more times I would ask that exact question.

"He wanted you to believe him dead," she said.

A brilliant flare of hope flickered to life deep within the sea of sorrow. "He...is he...?"

"Still alive, dear?" Mrs. Montford answered for me. "That...I do not know."

My heart sank, the bright hope dying like a doused ember.

"He left, hoping that if you ever learned the truth, you would never come looking for him. He insisted that everyone do what they could to make sure that you kept your distance."

"Why?" I asked. "Why would he want to push me away?"

"He never thought you would find out," she said. "It happened when you were so young."

"I saw him die!"

I hardly realized that I had stood to my feet, the liquid fire surging through my veins making my heart thunder in my ears, my vision tunneling.

Mrs. Montford stared at me sadly. "You were so small at the time. I am surprised such a memory would lodge itself in your mind."

"Why could you not have told me?" I asked, knowing somewhere in the back of my mind how far out of line I was stepping, but the anger pulsed within me like new blood, driving the concern from my mind. "Surely you could have done more to set this right than – than to give me an inheritance to make up for it?"

Mrs. Montford, aghast, stared as if truly seeing me for the first time.

I understood the feeling all too well. As far as I was concerned, the woman sitting in the chair before me was a complete stranger.

"Anna..." Jerome said. "It's – "

"No," I said with a wave of my hand in his direction behind me, sweeping a distinct line in the air between us. "No...I will not be dissuaded this time. I – I must know..."

I turned back to her, my eyes narrowing.

"If the Colonel did not kill him, what happened?" I asked. I could hear an edge to my words, a sharpness so poignant I might as well have shouted the question at her.

She winced as if I had. "He swam across the river and crawled out, as far as the Colonel told me," she said. "They had to make it believable, in case anyone happened to see it...which quite obviously, someone did." She gave me another wary look.

"He left me behind..." I said. "Surely he could have found some way to take me with him."

"I believe he wanted to," Mrs. Montford said. "He loved you more than his own life. I believe in his panic, he thought this to be his only choice."

My brow furrowed. "There is always another choice," I said, my hands curling into fists once more.

"Perhaps..." Mrs. Montford said.

"He cared so much for me that it did not matter that an orphanage had to be the one to take me in," I said, my past slowly unraveling and reweaving itself into a different, darker path. "I stayed alone in our home for almost a week before I was found and taken to the orphanage!"

Mrs. Montford's lips pursed. "We did not know of that until much, much later," she said. "The plan had always been for your aunts to take custody of you if anything were to happen to your father. They had both agreed to it at the time that he wrote up his will. We had known how to contact you after his death, but as we heard nothing, we assumed all was well. You would be brought up and protected by them. It was not until a mutual friend mentioned your name in a passing conversation five years ago that I began to think of you once more. I looked to see if I could write to you, simply to see how you were, and perhaps to share some memories with you."

"That seems awfully convenient," I said. "For so many years to pass with you not knowing my fate."

"It is the honest truth," Mrs. Montford said. "And that is our fault entirely. We had done as your father asked and kept our distance, hoping to keep the thugs who wanted your father dead at arm's length, in case any of them started to sniff around."

My heart hardened toward her.

"It had been years since we had heard from your father," Mrs. Montford said. "After the incident, we only heard from him three times...one of which was him asking us not to respond and apologizing that he would not be sending another letter."

"This all..." I began, shaking my head. "This is all...a great deal to – to take in..."

I sank back down into the chair behind me and felt the welcome pressure of Jerome's hand upon my shoulder, like an anchor grounding me to the reality of the moment.

"Your father wanted to give you a better life," Mrs. Montford said. "I know little of what became of him and have no knowledge of whether he was ever able to settle down anywhere. It is perfectly likely that he never stayed in any location for long. These men who were after him...had long memories. He assumed they would stop at nothing if they had any suspicions he was still alive. It was better to move the attention away from you."

I frowned. "Were you ever planning to tell me the truth? To tell me of his fate?" I asked.

Mrs. Montford's lips drew into a thin line. "No, dear," she said. "We never did."

My heart ached. *They lied to me for so many years...*

"As I said, it is what your father wanted," she said. "Granted, the circumstances changed a great deal when you were not taken in by your family. We wanted to do what we could to care for you, all the while still keeping to his wishes. It was difficult, as you can imagine, as we did not know what would be the best course of action. When we learned that you would soon be leaving the orphanage without having been adopted, I wanted to intervene, wanted to do something to help, to protect you in your father's stead..."

She shook her head.

"It was the only way I could think of without entirely giving away the truth."

"Why did you not simply tell me when you hired me?" I asked. "After all this time, my father may not even be alive anymore. So what good was it to keep his secret?"

Mrs. Montford's eyes narrowed slightly. "I feared for your safety. It was better for you to remain in the dark."

The anger boiled within me again. "I – " I said, and I held my tongue. Regardless of how I felt now, she was still my mistress and I still her maid. I might be able to get away with a great deal of what I had said but it was unwise to continue.

"I debated it all, more than you could know," she said. "The Colonel and I argued on a number of occasions about whether or not to tell you. He always wanted to but I feared for your safety...and truthfully, for our own. Years had passed without so much as a whisper from those criminals. I worried that if you knew, you might..." She looked down at her hands. "You might stir things up again. You might wish to go and find him and put yourself into danger."

I was angry. I wanted to rail against what she said, to argue that it was nothing more than a selfish decision...but I held my feelings in check. Her explanation was not unreasonable, I knew deep down, but I would not allow myself to admit it openly.

"The night the Colonel died..." she said. "I considered telling you. I do not know how much you recall of that evening, but – "

"I remember," I said. I had thought she was behaving rather odd, being as familiar with me as she was. *I suppose it makes sense, now.*

"Well, it is out in the open now," she said with a frown. "You know the truth."

"And there is nothing else I should know?" I asked.

"No," Mrs. Montford said. "Not a thing. That is everything. And I...I hope you will be able to forgive me one day."

My throat tightened and I looked away.

I would...but right now, I could not. Anger permeated through every thought. I needed time. I hoped she would allow me it.

"I do have your father's last letter..." she said, getting to her feet. "I think you should have it. If you want it, that is."

"I do," I said, knots snaking around my heart like thorny vines. "I should read his reasoning with my own eyes."

4

Colonel,

    Allow me to open this letter by apologizing for the months it has been since my last letter. As you might imagine, I have worried about sending any new information your way. The police may very well have never uttered your name but that does not mean I did not fear for you and your wife's safety. You are a resourceful man of influence, however, so I know that you will make do, which gives me great peace.

    And now, with Anna surely settled well, I can rest easy that any trace of her will have vanished. She is safe.

    I never knew how much I could miss someone...I hope that she remembers me as she grows.

    I have found my way to Italy, where I intend to stay for some time. I shall not give specifics of course, in case this letter is intercepted. I am hoping that my traveling is at an end, as I believe the place I have found is remote enough, and far enough, that my enemies will not be able to reach me here. The breeze coming from the sea is just what I needed...Perhaps you will have the chance to holiday here one day, and we might, by chance, cross paths.

I fear this will be my last letter. I cannot afford to endanger you any further. Thank you greatly for your help and your friendship. I wish that I had better wisdom and that the whole situation had turned out differently. Regardless, this is the fate I have found, and as such, I must make the best of it.

Farewell, friend. I hope you may one day forgive me for all the trouble I have put you through.

I looked up, squinting against the gusts of wind rushing up from the water below. The gales pelted against me, unconcerned if I stood as I did or not, effortlessly parting around me like snow melt down a river in warm, spring air.

Muscles in my legs began to ache from standing too long in one position and so I shifted my weight, turning around to survey my current circumstances.

I had never taken a ferry in all of my twenty-two years and never dreamed I would have the chance to take one across the English Channel as we were. Almost everyone had remained indoors, with the bite of the wind chasing them from the deck.

I cared not. I had been so lost in my thoughts for the last fortnight that very little troubled me outside of my own mind. Warm, cold, I did not mind.

In fact, the cold air had done a great deal to clear my cluttered mind...that was, until the letter from my father had crept in once again, dragging itself to the forefront.

I let out a heavy sigh, the wind tousling my hair into a brief cyclone above my head. I reached up and brushed it back down into submission before pulling the collar of my coat up around my face, nestling myself further into its warmth.

After agonizing over the letter, I had deduced that there were only a few places my father could have been referring to and the most likely of them seemed to be Venice. I knew little of the place, apart from the country in which it resided. Mrs. Montford told me that it was often referred to as the city of canals and that much of the city could be accessed by gondolas.

Mrs. Montford had immediately realized that I wanted to go there. She had a way of seeing right through me.

"I was hoping that I would find you out here..."

My heart skipped at the one voice I did not mind hearing right now.

I turned away from the roiling waves of the channel to see Jerome securing the door back inside the ferry behind him.

He strode over to the edge of the boat, coming to a stop right beside me. At once, I could feel the warmth of his nearness washing over me.

"It's been nearly an hour," he said in a low voice, his words tangling with the whistling wind.

It was not a question or an accusation...more of a simple statement, as if to remind me of the promise I had made, which was that I would return shortly.

"I apologize," I said. "I..."

"You do not need to explain," he said. "I realize you must have a great deal on your mind. All you have learned...it is more than anyone should have to try and come to terms with."

"I appreciate that," I said.

"Are you regretting your decision to make this journey?" he asked. "We do not need to take the train once we reach France, if you are wishing to go back."

I shook my head. "When I first read the letter, I almost decided to ignore it entirely. I wanted nothing to do with my father. I had lived most of my life without him and thought I could continue to do so. He had never tried to reach out to me, so why would I want to ever meet him again?"

I stared out over the water, the waves lapping against the steel side of the enormous ship we rode upon.

"However, as the days passed, I realized that I did want to search for him, if only for the reason that I wanted to ask him questions. There is so much I do not know, that Mrs. Montford could never explain. This is *my* life that I am seeking clarification on. If I ever want answers, this is the only way."

"You are quite brave, you know," he said, leaning against the rail on his elbows. He squinted against the wind rushing over the surface of the water. It rustled his auburn hair, reminding me of a bright, coppery flame. "I do not know if I would be able to trek as far as you have chosen to in order to meet with a father I had not seen in...well, almost twenty years."

I licked my lips, the cold having chapped them like bits of dry leather. "I do not know if it is bravery as much as fool-ishness," I said. "What if he is not there? What if I am entirely wrong about Venice?"

"Did not my aunt say that one of his previous letters had mentioned Venice?" Jerome asked.

"I suppose," I said. "What if this is nothing more than a fruitless trip, costing Mrs. Montford a great deal of needless money?"

"She is happy to spend it," Jerome said. "You do not understand the depth of her guilt over what happened to you. She feels deeply responsible for what you went through. She will probably be irritated with me for telling you this but she told me the thing she regrets most is that she did not try to find your aunts soon after your father's escape. She knows that if she had, then she and my uncle would have been able to rescue you from the orphanage long ago and save you much pain."

"I do not want her to think that any of this is her fault," I said. "That was never my intention..."

"It does not matter," Jerome said. "She would feel it regardless. She fears she has robbed you of a great deal by subjecting you to the life that you have been living under her care."

I said, "I wish that she had been the one to say these things to me."

"As I said...she would be none too pleased with me if she knew I was sharing this with you," he said.

It was kind of her. It was not her fault that the whole affair had ended the way it had.

"Well...what's done is done now. There is no changing the past," I said.

"Yes, but I think she means to help make a better future for you," Jerome said. "Which is why she insisted on this journey in the first place."

I allowed a few moments to pass, my mind lost in the swell of the waves around us and the whistle of the wind.

"Do you worry about the danger?" Jerome asked.

"No," I said, and knew that I meant it. "I am confident the worst of it is past. It probably faded long ago. Regardless of what his letters to the Colonel said, my father's distance from London has been more than enough for those old enemies of his to have moved on to some new target."

"I suppose so," Jerome said. "Though I do wonder how much they demanded of him..."

"It must have been more than I can possibly imagine if he was willing to fake his own death and..." I choked down the words *abandoned me* "...left me behind."

I shook my head.

"I realize the chance of actually finding him is slim but I want – " I tried to swallow, my voice catching in my throat. "I want to try, at the very least to assuage my own questioning spirit."

"You would likely never forgive yourself if you did not take this chance," Jerome said. "I have come to know you well enough to know that once your mind is made up, there is little that anyone can do to change it."

I could hear the hidden hurt behind his words, masked in what I knew he meant as a compliment, yet containing a true reflection of his heart.

"I am sorry that I went behind your back the way I did," I murmured. "With our last investigation."

Jerome shook his head. "There is nothing more than needs to be said. All that matters to me is that you are safe."

He said nothing else but I knew there was more and could see it behind his eyes.

The divide between us remained. Granted, considering what had happened with my father's letter, it had shrunk a great deal. But I still could not quite look at Jerome without hearing in my mind the argument we'd had over my recent involvement with the investigation into Mr. Murray's death. We had not yet had the chance to discuss the subject and now did not seem like the ideal time.

A rumbling horn blasted through the swirling gusts, sending my heart jumping and my body wincing...so strongly that I bumped right into Jerome's arm.

He laughed as I apologized.

"We must be arriving soon," he said. "Come on, let's get you inside to warm up for the last few minutes of the trip."

We made it to shore and to the station in due time and took the short ride from the coast to the city of Paris by train. On board, we enjoyed a lovely meal of poached rabbit and I admired the lilt to our conductor's voice.

"I have always loved the French accent," Mrs. Montford said as our trays were cleared away. "My cousin married a Frenchman, and every time they would come to visit for Christmas or during the summers, I would sit for hours and listen to her husband speak."

Jerome's brow furrowed as he stared down at his silver pocket watch. "I do not mean to alarm you, Aunt Bea, but are we not meant to catch the train to Venice at eight o'clock?"

"Yes, that's right," she said as she snapped open her handbag, withdrawing a small pocket mirror to examine her face after eating. Then her own brows wrinkled. "Why do you ask?"

He turned the clock face around to us. It was quarter 'til.

"Oh, good heavens," Mrs. Montford said, shoving the compact back within the purse. She gestured to the door. "You had best see where we are, Jerome. I shall not be pleased if we miss our train. It will be nigh impossible to find an open hotel this close to the station so last minute…"

Jerome rose and stepped out into the corridor. "Excuse me, sir?" he called as his voice disappeared after him.

Mrs. Montford's gaze shifted to me at once. "Are you all right? You have been rather quiet this trip, thus far."

"Yes, ma'am," I said with a nod.

She sighed, her eyes narrowing. "You know, I think upon our return home, we are going to need to be discussing how we will proceed from this point. I do not think that you are suited any longer to serving as – "

"We should be arriving in the next ten minutes," Jerome said, his head popping back into the compartment.

"Good heavens, boy," Mrs. Montford said, glaring up at him, her hand against her heart. "You frightened me half to death."

"My apologies," he said, slipping back inside and closing the door behind him.

I watched Mrs. Montford closely, not daring to ask her what she meant by what she had just said. *She does not think that I am suited any longer to serving as...what? I should not allow my thoughts to wander as they already try to, creating fantasies in which I will no longer be her servant.*

As Jerome began to pull the luggage from the racks near the door, and Mrs. Montford muttered to him about the possible solutions we might have to endure if we had missed the train, and how we might remedy it come morning, I pondered the possibilities of living in Mrs. Montford's London mansion...and not being a servant.

Which would make me...what?

It made little sense. If she were to allow me to stay, say until I turned twenty-five and was able to take the money the Colonel had left for me...then what would I do? Where would I go?

Perhaps it would be better for me to remain in her employ, I thought. *I have no shame working as a maid. I have enjoyed my life, if I am honest with myself. What could I possibly do instead?*

They were questions I did not have the strength to deal with now. The revelation of my father had been monumental enough, and as that was before me for the time being, I knew that I would have to focus on it entirely for now. It was only right...and best for my sanity.

The train came to a stop five minutes before eight, which sent Mrs. Montford into a tizzy.

"Do they not realize that some of us have connecting trains to catch?" she asked loudly as we hurried out onto the platform, sliding into a river of people as if we were salmon going upstream for spawning season.

"From what I understand, there was a bit of a problem with the engine," Jerome said.

"Oh, that is *wonderful,*" Mrs. Montford said. "To allow us to board a *faulty* train!"

I tried to remain close to Jerome as we wove our way through the busy station. It seemed a great many people were heading to other platforms, just as we were, knowing that Paris was one of the many great hubs for travel.

My heart skipped as I caught sight of the city out of one of the long rows of windows. I never thought I would ever see Paris, not with my own eyes.

As much as I wanted to stop and stare in wonder, my heart swelling with excitement, I stayed close to Mrs. Montford and Jerome, who gave the magnificent sight out of the windows only the briefest of glances before continuing on toward platform twelve, where we were to meet our train.

"Goodness me, goodness me," Mrs. Montford said. "I have not rushed like this since the year the Colonel and I took our trip to Germany to visit his uncle. We nearly missed our train from – "

"Aunt Bea, I do not mean to interrupt you but we must turn here," Jerome urged, taking her arm and guiding her down one of the halls to our right.

The babble of the passengers moving to and fro within the station hummed around me, in a variety of languages that I had only heard a few times in my entire life, even being in London as long as I had been.

I glanced at a large round clock jutting from the wall out over the passersby.

Two minutes past eight.

If this train was at all prompt, we were sure to have missed it.

I looked around and realized with a horrible sinking feeling that Jerome and Mrs. Montford had disappeared from my sight. The brief moment to look up at the clock had been enough to slow me down and separate me from them.

I spun around wildly, my eyes scanning the crowds that rushed past me for auburn hair or the olive green hat that Mrs. Montford had chosen for our journey.

Then I saw him; the very top of Jerome's head and eyes were fixed on me. He waved his hand wildly above the crowds.

With a twisting in my stomach as I realized how far they had made it without me, I started through the crowds...and my elbow collided with something hard.

"Look out, girl!"

I turned to see I had collided with an old woman's shoulder. She stood hunched over, hobbling through the platform in the same direction as I. She glared up at me over the top of her narrow spectacles, her hazel eyes flashing.

"Oh, ma'am, please forgive me," I said. "I have been separated from my party – "

"I will not hear your explanations," the woman spat. "I have a train to catch and I will not be delayed!"

"Are you going to Venice as well?" I asked.

"Yes," the woman responded but she hardly cared to stop, continuing on through the crowds that seemed to want to give her a wide berth. "Now, get out of my way!"

She waved the cane she held for support in my direction, nearly bringing it to meet my knees.

"Anna, are you – "

I looked up to see Jerome had managed to weave his way back to me.

"Young man, you really should not allow your wife to behave so poorly," the woman snapped. "She nearly knocked me over!"

"I am certain she did not mean to, ma'am, as we were separated – "

"That is not *my* fault, is it?" she spat.

With a huff, she trudged away from us.

Jerome turned to look at me, his expression puzzled. "Are you all right?"

"Yes, I believe so," I said. "That woman...I was so worried that I had lost you and – "

"It's all right," Jerome said, holding the crook of his arm out to me.

I slipped my hand in and he secured his own over the top of mine.

"I think she might be on the same train as we are," I said, a note of dismay in my voice.

"Perhaps," Jerome said. "But I would not trouble yourself too much. It is likely that we will not run into her again. On these overnight trains, you spend almost the entire time in your cabin."

"I hope you're right," I said, my heart sinking.

5

W e met Mrs. Montford at the corner of the hall, standing with our luggage.

"Is everything all right?" she asked, hurrying over to me.

"Yes," I said, though I struggled to keep my breathing steady. "We should hurry."

I could not explain exactly why the encounter with that woman troubled me as much as it did. Her sour expression had unsettled me, even if I had not done anything to harm her. She had looked at me as if I had personally attacked her or chosen to run into her. Why did that disturb me so much?

And why did it trouble me to think that she might be on the same train we were?

With a sinking feeling, I realized that the real reason I was worried was because I had been expecting trouble to appear and my interaction with her had been a whisper of the trouble I so dreaded.

I pushed that worry aside. It was entirely irrational. I

knew I was on edge because of the journey we were on and because I feared what I might find at the end of it.

That woman was nothing more than a self-fulfilling prophecy. I need to relax, lest my heart give out before we ever reach Venice!

The platform for our train was only another few steps away. My heart sank as I saw that it was almost entirely empty.

"Oh, no, have we missed it?" Mrs. Montford asked, slowing.

A face appeared out of one of the doorways of the train. His role as conductor was made plain by his uniform.

"Are you here for the eight o'clock?" he hollered out to us, cupping his hand around his mouth so that it might reach us.

"Yes!" Jerome exclaimed. "Have we made it in time?"

"Just so!" the conductor called. He hurried out onto the platform to meet us as we rushed forward. He scooped up my suitcase and tucked Mrs. Montford's beneath his arm.

"Thank you, sir, thank you," Mrs. Montford said as we stepped up onto the train.

"You are quite welcome," he said with a laugh.

The conductor was a slim individual with a thin, dark moustache. He stood ramrod straight with his heels together, reminding me of a penguin in his charcoal grey suit.

"You might have been the last passengers but you are most certainly not alone in being late! From what I have heard, a train from the coast arrived rather late?" he asked in his thick French accent. "Might I see your tickets?"

"Certainly," Jerome said, procuring them from his pockets. "And yes, the train we came in on did arrive late. I apologize for that."

The conductor took the tickets and gave them a scrutinizing look. "Uh, huh..." he muttered, swapping them around to inspect each one. "It is no trouble. As I said, you were not alone. The woman who boarded this train just a few moments before you is a regular of this particular trek and I often purposely hold the train a few moments later than usual, as I expect her."

I wondered if he was referring to the horrible old woman I had encountered earlier.

He moved so fast it was almost a blur. With a flash of his hand, he pulled a puncher from within his coat and swiftly punched two holes in each ticket before handing them back to Jerome. "There you are," he said with a smile. "Welcome aboard!"

"Thank you, sir," Mrs. Montford said.

"My name is Mr. Bedeau, the conductor of this train," he said. "If you would excuse me for one moment, I must signal to the engineer that we are ready to depart."

"Of course," Mrs. Montford said.

He walked to the door and took a bright lantern from a hook just inside the narrow hall of the train car. He slid the door open once more, leaned out, and gave an elaborate wave with the lantern grasped tightly in his hand.

The whistle of the train responded, and with a gentle lurch, the train began to move forward.

"Off we go, then," Mr. Bedeau said. "I shall show you to your compartment."

"Thank you," Mrs. Montford said.

"Sir, this woman you were speaking of," Jerome said. "The woman that arrived on the train just before we did? Was she an older woman with a bit of a hunch?"

Mr. Bedeau gave him a curious look over his shoulder, arching a brow. "Yes...though I suppose that might have been a few of our passengers..." His eye narrowed. "Why do you ask?"

"We passed a woman on our way here who seemed rather...irritable," Jerome said, giving me a brief glance. "We hoped that she was...well, all right."

Mr. Bedeau gave us an amused smile as we stopped at one of the doors between cars. "Oh, you are surely talking about Mrs. Clarkson."

He opened the door and the wind raced in through the doorway.

"Mind the gap!" Mr. Bedeau said as he effortlessly crossed the narrow space between the cars.

Jerome waited for me, holding my hand as I nervously crossed, even knowing that we would be safe, surrounded on all sides with sturdy rails of steel. The shifting of the train beneath my feet made my heart race, the thundering of the wheels as they continued to pick up speed. I clung to his hand so tightly that I worried I might crack some of the bones in his fingers.

It made it all the more frightening that we were going against the acceleration of the train. My balance shaking, I fought the urge to lean forward with the motion of the train itself, the momentum pulling me ahead.

Mercifully, we stepped into the next car, where the winds were silenced as the door locked closed.

"Yes, Mrs. Clarkson," Mr. Bedeau said, striding forward as casually as if we had not just been teetering outside in the cold night where anything might have gone wrong. "As I said, that must be who it was you met. I fear I must apologize, if you have already learned that she is rather disagreeable. That must mean that you have spoken with her?"

Jerome gave me another sidelong glance, to see if I wanted to answer.

"I very nearly collided with her in the station," I said. "She...well, she would not hear of an apology..."

"Typical," Mr. Bedeau said, shaking his head as we passed by compartment after compartment along the left side of the train, all of which were shut tight. "That woman will find any excuse at all to remain angry. I am certain that I have never seen her smile."

"A rather sad way to live, isn't it?" Mrs. Montford asked.

"I would assume so, especially given the lavish trips that she takes," Mr. Bedeau said. He shook his head. "Not that it is of any great surprise, is it? Her husband owned a portion of this railway and she has enjoyed the luxury of free travel for nigh on fifty years. I suppose it is only proof that money cannot buy happiness, eh?"

"Quite true," Jerome agreed.

Mr. Bedeau came to a halt at one of the compartments, the second to last one in the car. "Here we are, compartment 2B. Please, make yourselves at home."

He pushed open the door, and my jaw fell open.

It was by no means a palace, but when Mrs. Montford had explained our travel arrangements to me, I had imagined a pair of narrow bunks with perhaps a bit of fabric to cover the beds. Instead, I found what appeared to be a private compartment, with a bunk over each of the inward facing seats. A small door near the front stood open, revealing an incredibly small lavatory, but I could hardly believe there was one within the room at all.

"Well...it will do," Mrs. Montford said. "It will be crowded but, considering how late our tickets were purchased, this was the only compartment remaining." She glanced up at Jerome. "I suppose you shall have this bed and Anna and I will take these two on the right."

"Two?" I asked, looking around.

"Ah, the bench converts to a bed, you see," Mr. Bedeau said with a smile. "I shall be around to turn them down for you at ten o'clock, unless you would prefer them made sooner."

"No, ten shall be fine," Mrs. Montford said.

"Very well, I will leave you to rest," Mr. Bedeau said. "The dining car is car six. There will be a meal at nine o'clock and breakfast promptly served at seven before our nine o'clock arrival."

Mrs. Montford nodded. "Thank you, Mr. Bedeau," she said, as she nodded at Jerome.

He withdrew something from his pocket and pressed it into Mr. Bedeau's hand.

"Oh. Well, thank you, sir," the conductor said, pocketing the tip. "You are very kind. If you are in need of anything, simply press this button by the door." He pointed to a small brass fixture near the light switch. "I shall come around soon after. Enjoy your trip!"

With that, he pulled the door closed for us.

Mrs. Montford looked about. "It's a bit musty in here," she said. She walked over to one of the bunks and ran her hand over the blankets tucked tightly beneath the thin mattress. "It seems clean enough, though it would never be up to Mrs. Carlisle's standards..."

Jerome set about arranging the suitcases in the luggage area across from the small lavatory. "That Mr. Bedeau is a cheery fellow," he said. "Can't say I remember the last trip I met so personable a conductor."

"Yes, though it has been years since I have taken an overnight train," Mrs. Montford said.

Jerome glanced over at me. "And what do you think, Anna?"

"Yes, it is quite remarkable, these sorts of trains. I have never seen anything like it," I said politely.

Jerome's smile grew a bit wider. "I hope you are taking time to try and enjoy some of this trip."

"Yes, I do as well," Mrs. Montford said, her brow furrowing. "With how much you have been frowning these past few days, one might think we were off to a funeral."

"My apologies, ma'am," I said. "I will do my best to – "

"Good heavens, girl, you need not apologize for every little thing," Mrs. Montford said, shaking her head. "Jerome is right. You should try to enjoy some of this trip. It need not be all gloom. For goodness sake, we are going to Italy! Have you not ever wanted to see Italy?"

"Yes, ma'am, I have," I said. "I will try to do as you say and enjoy the trip."

Mrs. Montford's eyes flashed and she sighed. "Very well. I only hope that you are true to your word."

She turned to busy herself with her small bag, while Jerome finished settling his aunt's suitcase atop my own.

"It is surprising how the conductor already knew that woman I ran into," I said. "Mrs....Clarkson was her name?"

"Yes, I found that interesting, too," Jerome said, dusting his hands off. "I suppose one would not forget someone so abhorrent."

"Abhorrent, Jerome? Come now, you hardly met the woman for a minute," Mrs. Montford said.

"You would have thought so too, dear aunt, had you had the pleasure of speaking with her," Jerome said. "Don't you agree, Anna?"

"She certainly did seem a bit...sour," I said, voicing the word that kept rising up within my own thoughts of her. "I only hope you were correct, Jerome, that we shall not run into her again."

"Well, that may be difficult if we are to go to the dining car, unless she chooses to eat in her own compartment," Mrs. Montford said. "And speaking of the dining car, I am famished after all that rushing to the train. Shall we go and have ourselves a meal?"

After Mrs. Montford stepped into the lavatory to change into something more appropriate for dinner, we made our way back through the train, passing through each carriage until we made it to car six. I became a bit braver with each passing between the cars, as I gained surer footing and could anticipate the movement of the train beneath me. We passed through the day car, which was nothing more than long rows of seats, every other group facing the other, compartments without walls between them. Certainly nice looking, with clean floors and seats, but nothing particularly surprising.

The dining car, however, seemed to have been designed by someone else entirely. I wondered if it had been, perhaps, coupled with the wrong train entirely. A trio of small chandeliers hung from the center of the car, swinging gently as the train rumbled on. The seats had been coated in blue velvet. The servers wandered up and down the narrow aisle between the tables in handsome suits with bright, red cummerbunds.

"Ah, good evening, madam," said the server closest to us. He had a blonde moustache that had been waxed into a rather precarious twirl. "Might I interest you all in some coffee before dinner this evening?"

"That would be wonderful, yes," Mrs. Montford said.

He led us to a table along the left side, at the very end.

"I shall return shortly," the waiter said, absently retwirling his moustache around his finger.

"My word, this is a full train..." Jerome said, his eyes sweeping over the room.

He was correct. Almost every table had been filled and there had to have been fifty or more throughout the long car. A polished wooden bar stood in the center of the car, where another server stood making drinks for the guests.

I chanced a brief look up and down the tables and my heart sank as my eyes fell upon Mrs. Clarkson seated only a few tables away on the opposite side of the car.

A young child began to cry toward the front of the car. As late as it was, I could hardly blame the child. It must have been quite near to bedtime.

I noticed a young couple at a table two behind us, nestled between a rather boisterous group of businessmen who were busy playing a game of cards and an elderly couple who seemed intent on arguing under their breaths. The man kept trying to catch the young woman's gaze. I watched as she passed him a small smile, despite the noise. *Newly married, I would assume,* I thought.

A man extricated himself from his table and it took me a moment to realize that he was, indeed, one solitary man, as his width seemed to exceed what the chair he had left could handle. He sidled out from behind the table, bumping into the chairs behind him. His expression told me he was apologizing, as he squeezed himself back through to the aisle.

"Goodness..." Mrs. Montford said. "It is a busy evening."

"Yes," I said.

"We heard that this was going to be a full train," came a voice from beside us. "I suppose everyone is hoping for warmer weather in Italy!"

I turned to see the smiling face of a man at the table beside us. Hr was rather plain in his features but the woman sitting across from him was quite the beauty, as well as the young boy sitting quietly beside him, his nose buried in a book. The wife cradled an infant in her arms, rocking back and forth with a bottle full of warm milk held for the baby to drink.

"My apologies, I did not mean to eavesdrop," he said.

"No, no, it's all right," said Mrs. Montford. "It has been some time since I have taken an overnight train. I cannot remember them ever being so congested."

"The last time I took one, I must have been a boy," Jerome said. "It is a wonder how popular they have become."

"This is a fairly small train," the man said. "Often saved for those with last minute travel plans. We purchased tickets ages ago, taking a holiday from all the cold and grey weather."

"Who could blame you?" Mrs. Montford said. "February truly is one of the most dreadful times of year."

The man nodded. "Oh, I do apologize. My name is Mr. Richards. This is my wife and our children."

The woman smiled at us but it was clear that her focus was on the little one in her arms.

"I am Mrs. Montford and this is my nephew Jerome and his wife Anna."

I fought the urge to gawk at Mrs. Montford. *His wife? What could she possibly be thinking?*

"What a pleasant place to holiday, Venice," Jerome said with a warm smile, apparently unperturbed by his aunt's inaccurate description of our party.

"Oh, yes," said Mr. Richards, taking a sip from his coffee. "We have been looking forward to this trip for some time... though I can only hope that we have managed to get all of the frustrations out of the way early. Nothing can ruin one's peace and quiet like plans gone awry, yes?"

"That is quite true," Mrs. Montford said.

"What sort of trouble has occurred?" Jerome asked.

Mrs. Richards gave her husband a pointed look. "Come now, dear, they do not want to hear our woes."

Worry splintered within me like cracks through shifting ice. Woes? When their journey had only just begun? It sounded all too familiar.

"Did something happen here? On the train?" Mrs. Montford asked.

Mr. Richards stared at his wife and I could see the silent conversation passing between them. "My wife is right. I am certain that you would not want to hear our troubles."

"That's all right," Mrs. Montford said. "We have some time before dinner, and to be perfectly honest, I would not be at all unhappy to have a bit of distracting conversation in this rather boisterous room."

"Well, it certainly began as something worthy of a memorable trip," Mr. Richards said. "Our son Matthew loves trains. After speaking with the conductor, Mr....Oh, goodness, what was his name?"

"Mr. Bedeau?" Jerome asked.

"Yes, that's the man," Mr. Richards said. "We asked him if there would be any time for our son to meet the engineer. It was his one wish when we had told him we were taking the overnight train to Venice. We had arrived early with the hope it might be possible. Mr. Bedeau went to speak with the engineer and managed to find a short amount of time for some of the crew to show us around."

"Everything went well, until the conductor came in again while we were speaking with the engineer and the two began to argue," Mrs. Richards said, suddenly cross.

The baby in her arms began to fuss, its whimpering growing louder until Mrs. Richards adjusted the bottle and the baby settled back in.

"Argue?" I asked. "Argue about what?"

"It was something entirely inane," Mr. Richards answered. "I cannot even recall, but regardless, they raised a good deal of noise, frightening our son. We were none too pleased about it."

"It is unsettling to think the crew that is in control of the train is starting off on this journey so poorly," Mrs. Richards added, bouncing the baby who seemed a bit unhappier than simply being hungry would explain.

"I believe the matter was resolved but it did put a bit of a damper on the beginning of the trip," Mr. Richards said. He gave a pat on the head to his son, who barely looked up from the book in his hands, which I had only just realized had a picture of a gleaming, red steam engine on the front.

"I'm sorry to hear all that," Mrs. Montford said. "The conductor certainly seems like a decent fellow."

"Oh, I do not believe the problem began with him," Mrs. Richards said. "That engineer was rather cold and did not seem all too eager for our presence."

I glanced over at Jerome to find him watching me...but it was not with adoration, nor with anger. It was curiosity...the same I had begun to feel.

It seemed that we had stumbled upon yet another interesting place filled with interesting people. First Mrs. Clarkson, and then hearing of this squabble between Mr. Bedeau and the engineer...

Trouble in any shape and form, it seemed, had become fond of us.

"Well...enough about us," Mrs. Richards said, lifting the baby to lie against her chest to be burped. "Why are you three visiting Venice?"

"We are off on what I hope will be an equally pleasant

trip," Mrs. Montford said. "We are to visit the father of my nephew's new bride."

She then smiled proudly at me.

"Congratulations!" Mr. Richards said, nodding at Jerome.

"How wonderful," Mrs. Richards said, shifting her eyes to me. "When were you married?"

"Just a fortnight ago," Jerome said, lying as easily as if he were speaking the truth. "Anna's father was unable to make the trip, so we made a last minute choice to go and see him. We hope to surprise him."

"How lovely," Mrs. Richards said, beaming across the table at her husband. "And so recently wed. Oh, I wish the very best for you both. Marriage is so rewarding."

"Thank you very much, ma'am," Jerome said, inclining his head. He turned his gaze to me. "I cannot remember a happier time in my life."

Mrs. Richards nearly quivered with girlish delight. A romantic, quite obviously.

I was shocked at Jerome's willingness to go along with the ridiculous fib that Mrs. Montford had invented.

Then again, I realized it might be difficult to explain the true reason for our journey: that Mrs. Montford was taking her maid to search for her father, who had gone into hiding from enemies we couldn't discuss, her nephew accompanying us all the way.

Shouting behind us halted the conversation, as if someone had thrown the brakes on the train itself.

Whirling around, to my great dismay I realized that the angry voice had come from none other than Mrs. Clarkson.

"How *dare* you bring my food cold!" she bellowed, shoving away the plate that one of the servers must have only just placed before her. The beautiful ratatouille sloshed over the side of the pristine china, spilling out onto the white linen cloth, staining it bright red from the sweet tomatoes. "I do not even understand how it could *be* cold! You have only just brought it!"

"Ma'am, ma'am, please," the server said, hurrying to grab the plate before it went sailing over the opposite side of the table. "I made sure to bring you the very first plate, just as you asked – "

"I thought you would have *learned* by now," she screeched, tossing her napkin onto the table in disgust. "I should not think it so terribly *difficult* to comprehend! Or must I explain everything so thoroughly as to not be misunderstood?"

Every conversation around the car had died down and it seemed that every head had swiveled in her direction. It allowed her voice to carry further and her complaints to be more ridiculous.

"I do apologize, ma'am, I would be happy to speak with the chef and see if he might be able to prepare you a special portion – " the server began.

"No!" Mrs. Clarkson cried. She threw out her hands, the spoon in one hand flying free into the air.

It sung as it flew and struck the outside of a newspaper being held aloft by a rather sharply dressed businessman sitting in the table right across the aisle from her.

He lowered the paper, his eyes flashing as he regarded her. "Pardon me, madam," he said in a thick French accent.

"You will do no such thing!" Mrs. Clarkson carried on, ignoring the businessman entirely. "I will have a *fresh* meal. Leek soup, with haggis. And the chef will ensure that it is at my table within the next half an hour or he will have a great deal that he must answer for."

I looked over at the man that had been struck by the

spoon. With a huff, he folded his paper and arose from his seat, heading down the aisle toward the doorway.

"I shall speak to the chef right away, madam," the server said, and he rushed from the room.

Mrs. Clarkson must have been satisfied for the time being, for she folded her arms and went quiet, apparently untroubled by the stained tablecloth before her.

Other servers appeared a few moments later with carts laden with dishes and began distributing them among the tables. Conversation began to bubble up once more and the uneasy air began to dissipate.

Jerome leaned across the table, dropping his voice low so only his aunt and I could hear him.

"I certainly hope that cranky old woman is not in the compartment beside ours," he murmured. "I fear we shall not sleep a wink if the bed is not up to her standards."

Mrs. Montford watched the woman with her usual sharp gaze, and I could only nod glumly.

6

My chest burned. My lungs screamed for air. I wanted nothing more than to part my lips and draw in cold gulps of air.

But I could not.

Light glimmered in the distance. I knew it meant life. I knew it meant rescue.

I urged myself forward but it was as if my own body fought against me. *Why bother? You will never reach it.*

I had to try.

As slowly as if I had fallen into molasses, I dragged myself forward. As if I had been shrouded in shadows of great and terrible weight, my knees buckled beneath me and my back groaned with pressure.

Darkness seeped into the edges of my vision, threatening to swallow me up. I fought it back, my eyes focused on the light.

Just...a little...further.

I stretched out my hand, the muscles in my arms fighting me, my whole body shaking with the effort –

I gasped and my eyes snapped open.

Sitting up straight, my mind swam with fear, the blood surging through my ears.

I blinked and stared around, my eyes adjusting to the darkness around me.

The only glimmers of light I could see were flashes. It took a moment for my mind to fully understand that it was not so much flashing as it was moving and swiftly. With a nervous gulp, I realized it was a window.

I rubbed my eyes with the heels of my palms, trying to focus. I drew in deep breaths, trying to slow my frantic heartbeats. I had never realized how I had taken breathing so terribly for granted.

It had been a dream. Nothing more.

It did not surprise me at all that the dream had been about my father...and the night that he had been killed.

Pretended he had been killed, I reminded myself. I knew that was going to take some getting used to.

I started as a realization struck me.

I had not been dreaming from my own perspective. The burning in my chest, the inability to breathe.

Understanding resonated within me, like a troubled pond growing calm.

I was dreaming...as if I were my father swimming for his life.

The longer I sat there and thought of it, the more details resurfaced in my mind. The golden embroidery of the Colonel's coat, the splash of the water that I finally realized lacked a distinct gurgling sound. Perhaps the clearest thing was the hasty apology that was whispered before I was submerged beneath the water.

I knew that last part might have been my own mind trying to make sense of the whole situation but it was not entirely out of the realm of possibility. The Colonel had played his role well and only did so out of friendship.

The sticky fear began to melt away as my heart calmed. It was nothing more than a dream...but a much better dream with a much better ending than anything I had suffered through for the majority of my life before this.

*I will be able to heal, now, from those terrible nightmares...*I thought.

Somehow, the thought in and of itself was freeing. A weight that I had grown entirely accustomed to, that had wedged itself somewhere deep within my heart, dislodged itself and faded away.

I allowed the dream to fade with it and just listened. I had grown used to the sounds of the city at night, which had taken some time after living in the quiet, secluded estate in Maidstone. The rhythmic hum and *clu-clunk* sounding beneath me reminded me that I was not, in fact, in London still.

When I opened my eyes once more, I could see the room a bit more clearly.

I was sitting up in the top bunk of the train compartment in the overnight train. Peering over the side, I could just make out Mrs. Montford's shape beneath the quilt in the bunk below. The steady rise and fall of her chest gave me some relief. Not only had I not woken her but she was also all right.

How long will it be before that is not the first thought that crosses my mind?

My eyes swept across to the other side of the compartment, where Jerome had tucked himself into the upper bunk across from my own.

My heart stirred within me, and as I lay my head back down upon my pillow, I shifted just so I might be able to see him.

I thought back to earlier that evening in the dining car,

when he had so easily gone along with Mrs. Montford's fib about the two of us being newlyweds. How had he been so willing to go along with the story? And why had she felt secure enough to share it with complete strangers?

The thought was too much for me for the time being and so I rolled back over onto my back.

Staring up at the ceiling, I allowed myself to be lulled by the motion of the train. Vaguely, I wondered where on our journey we were.

Icy worry snaked into my heart once more as I thought about the new situation that I had found myself in.

Meeting my father again...but knowing that it would truly feel as if it were happening for the first time.

I knew that it would be some time before I would be able to find sleep again. I did not want to wake Jerome or Mrs. Montford by rolling around on the slim bunk. As quietly as I could, I slid down to the floor, and snatching up my thick robe, I wrapped myself up and stepped out into the hall.

The wheels were louder out in the hall, nothing more than a wooden floor and the steel wall of the train to muffle them. They continued onward, ever onward.

I glanced up and down the hall. To my great relief, I was entirely alone. I let out a long, heavy sigh and leaned against the wall.

I knew that I should be resting, given the fact that we would be doing a great deal of searching come the morning, once we reached our destination. I had no idea what all that might entail or what it might take to find my father. Seeing the situation now, this close to our arrival, I realized just how fruitless the whole endeavor might be.

What if we did not find him? What if this was nothing more than a waste of time?

Would Mrs. Montford be angry with me for going through all of it?

That was not what frightened me, however...not really.

What would I do if we did manage to find my father?

I had not seen him since I was six years old. He had died before my very eyes...or at least, so I had thought...

What would he think of me? Would he be excited? Would he be upset? Had he missed me like I had missed him?

I bit down on the inside of my lip and turned to begin a slow pace down the hall. I needed to tire myself out so I could return to our compartment and get back to sleep. I knew that I would be exhausted come morning if I did not. I simply needed to distract myself, to think of something else –

The door at the far end of the hall opened and I nearly jumped out of my skin. I wheeled around and saw Mr. Bedeau enter the car, carrying a lantern in one hand in which a small light flickered, casting a warm pool of light around him.

"Oh, good evening, mademoiselle," he said, smiling at me. "Or, should I say, almost morning, yes?" He chuckled, his lantern swinging at his side.

I let out the sharp breath I'd drawn and tried a rather nervous smile. "Yes, sir...thank you. Good morning to you, as well."

"Awfully late," he said, striding toward me, peeking at the doors of the compartments as he passed by them. "Is everything all right?"

"Oh – " I said, my face flushing. "Yes, of course. Just can't sleep."

"Ah, yes, had many of those nights myself," he said, stopping a short distance away and smiling at me. "Is everything in the compartment to your party's liking?"

"Of course, sir," I said. "We are very pleased."

He nodded. "Very good. And is there anything that I can get for you? Perhaps some warm milk from the dining car? Or a spot of tea?"

"No, sir," I said. "Thank you very much, though, for the thought."

"Well, I do not mean to be rude but I shall be on my way. I need to check on the rest of the cabins before turning in myself."

"Certainly. Do not let me keep you," I said, withdrawing against the wall.

He tipped his conductor's hat before passing by me.

I watched him go, as he inspected each door, leaning near them to see if anyone was still awake.

Soon after, he disappeared through the door at the other end of the car and silence fell once more.

I sighed, looking around, the echoes of hurt and worry still weighing heavily upon my heart. The distraction had been welcome, whether I had expected it or not, for it had given me the chance to be outside of my own thoughts for a few moments.

I glanced over my shoulder at the door, my mind shifting gears to entering the cabin once more, worrying about waking Jerome and Mrs. Montford. I hoped that in my tired state, I would be able to tread carefully through the dark, avoiding banging my knee or perhaps bumping Mrs. Montford's bunk as I climbed the narrow ladder to my own.

I steadied myself and reached out for the door to the compartment when the same door to the car slid open again.

"Oh, I beg your pardon, Miss," said the man who

entered, ducking his head. "I did not think anyone would be awake." His accent indicated that he was a Frenchman, like Mr. Bedeau, and his uniform painted him as one of the train workers. Perhaps an engineer, given the smears of coal across the front of his uniform and the bridge of his nose. When he tipped his dark hat to me, I noticed the edges of dark hair peeking out from beneath it.

This certainly is not as quiet a place as I might have expected, in the middle of the night...

"It is no trouble," I said, drawing my robe more closely around my shoulders.

I reached for the door to my compartment once more.

"Begging your pardon, Miss, but did you by any chance happen to see the conductor move through here?"

I looked over at him and noticed the trouble in his green eyes. He lacked the same cheeriness that Mr. Bedeau had. I felt a small hitch of fear. *Perhaps there is something wrong with the train?*

I did my best to smother the idea. I would never sleep if I allowed that thought to run wild.

"I did, sir, yes," I said, and pointed down the hall. "He passed through here, not more than a few moments ago. He cannot be far ahead."

"Thank you," he said, and continued on past me without another word before disappearing through the door.

My brow furrowed. Something was not at all right.

I turned and made my way back into the cabin, finally.

The darkness pressed in around me, the only lights coming from the distance out through the window. The continuous *clu-clunk* of the train along the track was rhythmic enough that my eyelids had begun to grow heavy once more.

With great care, I tucked my robe away into my suitcase,

and nestled my slippers underneath the bench before climbing the ladder.

I snuggled back underneath the somewhat disappointing, thin quilt before letting out a sigh, allowing the tension and stress of the rest of the evening to fade away. Now, the only thing that I needed to do was worry about rest.

Except my mind still wanted to work. I pondered over the engineer's worried expression, and I reflected back to the conversation we had had at dinner with that family on holiday to Venice. The wife had said that the engineer and Mr. Bedeau had an argument in front of them. While Mr. Richards had not been terribly concerned, Mrs. Richards had been troubled by the whole affair. I could not quite forget her comment about how she worried about the crew taking care of the train we all rode upon being at odds with one another.

It troubles me too, if I am honest with myself.

A subtle snoring nearby caused me to turn my head, and my eyes fell upon Jerome once more. He had not moved at all during the time I was out in the hall.

I smiled, in spite of my worry. He was sleeping so peacefully...

Part of me was rather jealous that he could do so.

I sighed, sinking back into the mattress.

Part of me wished that I could simply hide beneath this blanket forever, never having to face the light of day again. It would certainly be an easier life, would it not? No responsibilities, no awkward conversations...no estranged fathers to meet.

I knew full well that I did not need to go on this trip. I could have gotten on perfectly fine without ever having left London, without pursuing the possibility of him still being alive. I had lived the past sixteen years without him and had learned how to get on well enough, hadn't I?

I should not lie to myself. A large reason why I am dragging my feet is because I worry that he left so easily and never tried to come back because he...

My throat grew tight and I pinched my eyes shut. It was even difficult to think the thought through.

...Because he did not care about me.

I knew how foolish that was. How could a father possibly stop loving their child?

Then why did he leave me?

It was the question I could not answer. No matter what reason I came up with, no matter what conclusion I came to, nothing I could think of was good enough to leave a child behind.

Why would he not want to try and get through it with me? Why would he not have tried to reach back out to me? Would it not have killed him to be away from me?

The ache that settled over me seemed almost worse than the ever-present scar that had been in my heart since his supposed death. There were so many years that had passed, time we could have been together...

I shut my eyes and tried to settle myself down.

Before I was able to get at all comfortable, before I was able to force myself to think of something better and happier...my heart nearly leapt through my chest when the sound of a terrible scream echoed from out in the hall.

7

I sat straight up, my head snapping around toward the door.

"Good heavens..." came Mrs. Montford's voice, along with the rustle of blankets. "What was that?"

Jerome's head lifted from his pillow.

Another scream caused him to throw the covers aside and leap down to the ground.

He reached for his robe, which he had still folded in the top of his suitcase. Throwing it on, he looked over at us.

"Stay here," he said, tying the velvet tie around his waist. "I shall go and see what – "

Another scream.

He did not wait. He slid the door open and dashed out into the hall.

"Anna, are you here?" Mrs. Montford asked.

I slid down the ladder, grabbed her robe from her trunk, and opened it for her as I stood beside her bed. "It's all right, Mrs. Montford. Jerome has gone out to see what is wrong."

More screams came from out in the hall as Mrs. Montford rose to her feet.

"My word, are we in danger?" Mrs. Montford asked.

My heart hammered in my throat as I stared out into the hall, willing Jerome to come back into sight.

As soon as she was dressed properly, I hurried to the compartment door and stared out, my eyes sweeping from left to right.

The family in the compartment beside us peered out, the father holding his arm out wide to keep a curious young boy contained near their car, the mother staring with her hand clapped over her mouth.

When I finally looked down the hall, in the direction that Mr. Bedeau and the engineer had gone earlier, my heart crashed to the floor beneath my feet.

The cranky old woman who had made the scene at dinner stood out in the hall in a thick dressing gown and matching nightcap, head held in her hands, trembling. A man, also in his night clothes, stood beside her, his hand resting on her shoulder. His head, however, was turned and his gaze fixed on the very reason why she must have been screaming in the first place.

Mr. Bedeau lay prostrate on the floor, his head bent at a strange angle pushed up right against the wall. His lantern looked as if he had tossed it, lying on its side near the door leading out to the next car.

I closed my eyes and sunk back into the compartment, the poisonous tendrils of fear creeping up my throat once more, spreading through every inch of my being.

"What is it?" Mrs. Montford asked. "What happened?"

"The conductor..." I murmured. "I think he might be dead."

All of the color drained from her face. "He...is dead? But how?"

I shook my head.

She hurried to my side and peered out into the hall, and the gasp that soon followed told me all I needed to know about her thoughts.

"And Jerome!" she exclaimed. "He is over there, as well."

I looked out and could hardly believe I had missed him, standing there next to the motionless body of Mr. Bedeau. Two other men stood with him, one on either side. The one to his left nodded his head as Jerome spoke, and the other peered down at Mr. Bedeau.

"Why is no one helping him?" I asked without a great deal of thought. "Why are they allowing him to lie there like that?"

"Anna, dear..." Mrs. Montford said in as gentle a tone as she could muster.

"I do not see any blood," I said, my eyes sweeping up and down the hall, looking for any signs of a struggle. I could not look away if I wanted to, and with the same sick fascination that I had felt every other time I had been in the direct presence of a corpse, I searched for evidence, all the while knowing that if I found it, I would never be able to forget it. It would be forever seared into my thoughts, but it would certainly not be the first time.

"No blood?" Mrs. Montford asked.

"No," I said.

"Is it possible that he is – he is only injured? Perhaps has lost consciousness?"

I watched as Jerome knelt down beside the conductor. He gave him a quick look over before standing once more and saying something to the man beside him.

"What happened?" asked the man in the room next to ours. "We heard someone screaming."

"I do not know," I said, drawing my robe more tightly around myself.

"Is he all right?" the man asked.

I thought it might be clear that he was not all right, but it was easier to deny the obvious truth right before our eyes than to admit that someone might have died right outside our rooms in the middle of the night.

"I do not know..." I said.

I noticed the boy standing behind him, looking frightened.

"Perhaps you should get the boy back to bed," I said with a pointed look at the father. "I am certain that Mr. Bedeau will receive the care he needs."

Even as I spoke the words, I knew them to be a lie. Did that make it wrong if it was to protect the mind of one so young?

"Very well," the father said, and he turned to his son.

I heard the protest, but with nothing more than a firm word from the boy's mother, he turned around and went inside.

I hoped there were no other children around. This was something I had not yet had to factor into these situations.

"Come on, folks, please," came a voice down the hall. "Everyone back inside, there is nothing you can do out here."

A young man in the same uniform as the engineer who had passed through earlier waved people back toward their cabins, though none of them were listening to his chastising. His features betrayed the fear he felt and his efforts were none too great to usher people from the crowded, narrow hall.

"Here, of all places?" Mrs. Montford muttered behind me.

I turned to see her sitting on the side of her bunk, staring down at her hands. She looked up when I walked back over to her and sat down on the edge of the bench beneath Jerome's bunk.

She tried to give me a smile but it turned immediately into a frown as she shook her head. "How could this happen?" she asked. "Again? How is it that these terrible events continue to occur around us?"

I blinked at her, pondering what she had said. She had put the both of us together into one situation...as if we were equals.

I wrestled with the uncertainty of what changes might become of our relationship upon our return to London and instead tried to focus on the moment before us.

"I do not know," I said. "What I do know is that it has not helped me to ask that question. Instead, I have realized that I have been given a unique opportunity to help others find peace, even perhaps at the cost of my own."

I glanced toward the door, hearing the low murmuring from Jerome outside. He would return when he was ready. I did not need to rush him.

"Whether or not I like these circumstances, I have been placed in them, and I believe it might be for a reason," I continued. "Perhaps I can endure them better than someone who has little experience with death, and as such, I am able to assess these matters with a keener eye and with some objectivity. I can think of the deaths that I have had to witness...or I can realize that I have been the one to find the persons responsible and help bring them to justice."

I heard someone hurry past the open door of the compartment, and turned just in time to see the young engineer run by, likely heading back toward the front of the train.

I gave Mrs. Montford a tight smile.

"Perhaps none of this makes sense..." I said. "To be honest, it hardly makes sense to me, either. I simply know that if I can have any sort of control in these rather uncontrollable situations, then I feel less frightened."

Mrs. Montford pursed her lips and looked out into the hall expectantly.

"Well..." she said, heavily. "I suppose I had not considered it in such a way. You have endured these terrible deaths more than I have, and I have dealt with my fair share. If you have wanted to do what you could to make sense of it all, then I certainly cannot blame you."

She frowned as she looked back at me.

"I assume that the conductor...that he is – "

I nodded. I knew there was little chance that he would still be alive, given the strange angle of his neck and the way his body sprawled across the floor. I could only hope for his sake that his death had come swiftly...

"Well, I do not suppose there will be a great deal of sleeping the rest of the night," she said, glancing down. "It is not as if these mattresses are of any use. They might as well have put a slab of wood down and thrown a blanket atop it. These old bones notice such things the older I get, the more unpleasant it becomes to simply sit or sleep."

"I am sorry, Mrs. Montford," I said. "I would be happy to go out and see what Jerome has found if you wish to try and rest more."

"No, I do not think I could sleep if I wished to," she said, her brow furrowing. "Though I do wonder what Jerome has found. I cannot imagine that the conductor might have fallen and died in such a way by accident."

"No, I do not imagine that to be so, either," I said. "Sadly, I think that someone very likely killed Mr. Bedeau."

Footsteps in the hall forced me to cut off any other words I might have said.

"I am going to check to see if anything is happening," I said, and rose, crossing the narrow compartment to the door.

"Be careful," Mrs. Montford said. "Your father would never forgive me if you were somehow injured on our way to see him…"

I swallowed. How could she speak so freely about my father when we had never spoken of him before I learned the truth? Did she not see it would take me time to become so comfortable with the idea?

"No, I did not see anything!"

It was the cranky old woman, and she spoke in a sour tone to one of the men who had been standing with Jerome. Her face, splotchy with anger, turned up to him, as she prodded him in the chest with the end of her boney finger.

"I left my room to make my way to the dining car," she went on. "As old as I am, I can hardly sleep as it is! You would not know anything about that, though, would you?"

"You are the only one who saw him," the man said apologetically. "All I wanted to know is if you had seen anyone else."

"No, I did not see anyone else!" she screeched. "If I had, do you not think I would have said as much?"

Jerome's eyes flashed, and he looked down the hall to where I stood. He gave me a pointed look and nodded his head.

"What about all these other onlookers?" Mrs. Clarkson said, turning to look out over the others congregated down the hall. More guests had appeared near the back door, obviously having heard of the commotion in the further car. They looked as worried as the others, peering around one another at the body that Jerome tried to block by standing in front of. "What if any of them saw something?"

Jerome pursed his lips, but lifted his chin and spoke loudly enough that his voice carried down the hall. "Did anyone see anything?" he asked. "Anything at all?"

He seemed to be taking charge of matters, perhaps because no one else had stepped forward to do so. It made sense, given his previous involvement in police investigations of mysterious deaths.

"It was likely someone in this car!" Mrs. Clarkson squealed. "That leaves only four families!"

My face flushed. How could she be sure?

Jerome shook his head. "Whoever attacked him clearly has to be on this train but it could have been anyone, as they could have easily slipped out. It is unclear how long he has been lying here. We will have to find out how recently anyone saw him alive."

"Alive?" I heard behind me.

"Does that mean he is – "

"How could this be?"

"Who could have done such a – "

"Please remain calm," Jerome called, trying to speak over the rising din.

Many of the voices did fall silent, eyes turning to him.

"Did anyone see him within the last few hours?" Jerome asked.

No one spoke up for a few moments.

My heart began to pound uncomfortably in my ears.

"I saw him after dinner," said the husband in the compartment beside ours.

"The last time I saw him was when we boarded the train," said another man near the door, likely from one of the other compartments.

"I do not recognize him at all," said a woman behind him, struggling to keep back tears. "The poor, poor man..."

I licked my dry lips, my tongue still somewhat mossy from sleep. "I...I saw him," I said, looking directly at, and speaking directly to, Jerome. "Not long ago, shortly before Mrs. Clarkson's scream."

8

I could feel every eye in the train turn toward me, and for the length of a few heartbeats, all I could hear was the consistent chug of the train.

At once, I realized my mistake. I should never have said a word. Now, without a doubt, everyone on the train would think that I was the one who killed him, even though I knew full well that I was not.

I had not yet been accused of murder myself. Not once, in all of the investigations I had done, had I ever found myself in a compromising situation. How could I have known that leaving my compartment and accidentally running into Mr. Bedeau would then lead me to being in a suspicious place?

"You saw him alive?" Jerome asked, his brow furrowing. "So recently?"

I nodded, as more eyes turned to me. "He – he was making his final rounds of the evening, passing by each compartment to see if they needed anything before he turned in," I said.

The uproar happened immediately.

Mrs. Clarkson, leading the way, began to assault me with questions. "What in the world were you doing out of your compartment so late, girl?"

That was quickly followed by others with echoing sentiments.

"How can we trust her? How can we be sure that she is not the one who killed him? Lock her up!"

The red in my face deepened, blood pumping in my ears and forehead.

"Easy now, everyone, let's calm down," Jerome said. "Simply being one of the last to see him doesn't make her guilty."

"How can you know that?" the husband from the compartment beside us asked, his brow furrowing with worry. "How can we be certain of anything you say? How can we trust that *you* were not responsible?"

It was becoming clear to me that fear was getting the better of everyone the longer they gave themselves up to the reality of the situation. Questions begot questions and they became more accusatory, more suspicious as the moments ticked by.

Jerome held his hands up, trying to speak over the crowd, but the man who had spoken yelled even louder, pointing his finger in Jerome's direction, spittle flying from his lower lip.

"This is madness!" protested another man from the door of the compartment at the end of the hall. I recognized him as the businessman who had been reading the newspaper at dinner when Mrs. Clarkson had thrown her spoon in anger. "How can you all accuse this man who is doing his best to discover what actually happened?"

That seemed to reach a few, for they quieted down.

"And who is he, exactly?" asked the man near us, his voice coated in suspicion.

"As it happens, I'm someone who's had experience dealing with matters like this," Jerome said. "I have sometimes assisted police investigations."

"Like a private investigator," said the businessman, nodding. Not only was he well-dressed, but even handsome in his night clothes, a matching set of silk pajamas.

The man in the compartment beside ours seemed to take the information seriously, for he snapped his mouth shut.

"How convenient that you happen to be riding this train," remarked the woman in the compartment beside us. Her tone was decidedly skeptical.

"It is purely by chance, I assure you," Jerome said. I could see that he knew his words might fall on deaf ears but he did not seem to mind too terribly much. "I, myself, have not seen Mr. Bedeau since he walked us to our compartment earlier this evening. Regardless – regardless," he said, raising his voice as more protests rose from the crowd. "We know that whoever it is that is responsible is *on this train.* The best thing we can do is find who it is, and so I need anyone to tell me anything that they found suspicious tonight. I shall start with the young woman who saw him last."

At first, I wondered why he seemed to be avoiding revealing the fact that we knew one another, but then I realized that it might not be terribly advantageous for him to do so right now, with the suspicions people had of me. It was best for me to cooperate and set the example for everyone else on the train.

"I was not the only one who saw him," I said, continuing my story. "I am certain that others must have, given that he

was making his rounds through the rest of the train. After
he came through, a short time later, just a few mere
minutes, I believe an engineer came by, looking for him."

Jerome's gaze sharpened. "The engineer?"

I nodded. "He said he was looking for Mr. Bedeau." I
held my tongue about the concerns I had about the engineer and the nervous way he had hurried on through the
train car.

"Where did Mr. Bedeau happen to go?" Jerome asked.

I pointed toward a door.

"Through there," I said. "After the engineer went after
him, I do not know what happened. I returned to my
compartment."

"What were you doing in the hall that late in the first
place?" asked the man from the next compartment.

I flushed but felt it best to be honest in this situation. "I
was having trouble sleeping after...well, after a nightmare."

Even I could hear the sincerity in my own voice, and the
man asked no further questions, which gave me hope that
he believed me.

"I have an idea," Jerome said. "It would make these next
steps a great deal easier for everyone. I would ask everyone
to make their way to the dining car, as we cannot all stand
here in this hall. Does this sound agreeable?"

Murmurs spread through the compartment, and I could
see that his suggestion had been a wise one, despite making
everyone else reluctant.

"All right, you heard the man," said the other young man
dressed in a crew member's uniform. "Let's be on our way.
File through the door, that's it..."

He began to usher everyone toward the door.

Mrs. Montford appeared at my side, peering out into the
hall. "Well..." she murmured, watching people disappear

back through the door at the end of the car. "I suppose we should follow suit, then..."

Jerome stepped up to our compartment, watching the others filing away. "Are you both all right?" he asked.

When I looked up into his face, my heart skipped a few beats as I saw the confidence had disappeared, replaced with a younger, more nervous expression. He had appeared so firmly in control, when in actuality, it seemed that he was doing his best to keep himself calm so as to help everyone else feel the same.

I said nothing, though. He needed to appear strong, even if I knew that he was as shaken by all of this as the rest of the passengers on the train.

"I had not realized that you had even slipped out of the compartment," Jerome said in a low voice, watching people at the other end of the car. "I must have been sleeping harder than I thought."

"I did my best not to wake either of you," I said.

"You had a nightmare?" Mrs. Montford asked.

"Yes," I said. "It is nothing important, of course. Just...I can hardly remember it now, given all this."

Her eyes narrowed slightly but she did not press me any further.

"What did Mr. Bedeau say to you? Did you speak with him?" Jerome asked.

"Briefly," I said. "He asked if I was all right, and told me he was checking on the passengers, just as I said. He wanted to know if our compartment was to our liking. That really is all."

"And the engineer?" Jerome asked.

"Looking for Mr. Bedeau," I said. "I know nothing else."

Jerome's brows furrowed. "Well, I believe that unless

someone else knows something in the dining car when we arrive, then we should go and speak with that engineer."

"Those were my thoughts, precisely," I said.

An angry voice behind us caused me to look over my shoulder.

"No, absolutely not," said the businessman in the silk pajamas. His arms were folded and he glared at one of the servers who had come in amongst all the chaos.

"But sir, you cannot stay here. We must all go to the dining car."

"And leave my compartment?" the man asked, aghast. "Certainly not. I am not going anywhere in the middle of the night."

"But sir, you were the one who tried to convince everyone to listen to the investigator – " the server said.

"But that does not mean that *I* have to go," he snapped. "*I* am not responsible! Why should anyone expect me to leave my compartment when there is a killer on the loose?"

"Tensions are quite high," Jerome murmured to us in a low voice. "Come along...I know where he is if we need to speak with him."

We made our way from the car, back through the others lined with compartments, almost all of which were empty. The closer we drew to the dining car, the more confusion I saw. I heard an infant crying through one compartment, and through another partially cracked door saw a family scrambling to dress in a hurry. Passing by another, a man and woman were arguing while the man tugged on a jacket. With a small jolt, I realized that they were the couple who had been staring lovingly at one another that evening, despite all the chaos around them.

We reached the dining car a few moments later and it

shocked me to see it as full as it was. The cacophony within was something I could have done without.

Jerome looked around. "Perhaps this was not such a wise idea..."

He was not wrong. Not only was every seat taken but it was clear that everyone in the train was not at all pleased to have been awoken. I realized quickly that there might not have been any reason to have *everyone* come to the dining car. The truth was that there really were only a few who could have killed Mr. Bedeau, if they had worked with him. Which made me realize...

"Jerome," I said, reaching up to gently touch him on the upper arm.

"Yes?"

"It is very likely that whoever killed Mr. Bedeau knew him," I said, turning away so that those nearby might not be able to read the words on my lips. "I feel foolish that the thought has not struck me until now, but given the hour, I suppose I can blame it on exhaustion."

"I imagine you are right," Jerome murmured. His eyes swept over the room. "There are those who need not be here, people who I know for certain just by seeing them now are not the ones."

Resolve straightened his shoulders as he hopped up onto the nearest bench and then up onto the table. He held his hands high and looked out over the crowd.

"Ladies and gentlemen, I must apologize," he said. "In the confusion of all that has happened, I did not make myself clear. One member of each family from each cabin should suffice for briefing and questioning. I will not ask the mothers and the young children to sit here any longer. Please, return to your compartments and allow the children to sleep. When we have found answers, I will be certain that they reach you."

I watched as the families began to gather themselves up once more. At a table nearby, I saw one older girl, who might have been ten or eleven, scoop a blubbering infant from her mother's arms and start after her three younger brothers, their mother guiding them along toward the door like a group of ducklings. Further ahead, I watched as an older brother hoisted a toddler up over his head to rest on his shoulders, while a pair of twins, no older than five or six, dissolved into tears.

We waited a few moments for nearly three quarters of the room to clear out. Soon all that was left was a large group of angry looking men and those who must have been traveling alone.

It impressed me that everyone had stayed without a great deal of verbal complaints.

"Very good," Jerome said as the last young lad was escorted from the room, head hanging, blanket clutched tightly in his little fist. "All right. Thank you, to all of those who have agreed to remain here."

"Is it true?" called one of the men, a surly looking, broad-shouldered fellow. "That the conductor is dead?"

Jerome dipped his head, clearing his throat. "I see that you gentlemen see no reason to delay. Yes, Mr. Bedeau is dead. I believe he has been killed."

I found myself grateful that the children had vacated the car. These were conversations they truly did not need to hear.

"Killed? Do you mean murdered? How do you know?" asked another man.

"Who are you?" came another question.

"My name is Jerome Townson and I have assisted the

London police in a couple of criminal matters. I, and my partner who is on this trip with me, have spent a great deal of time doing what we can to resolve issues like this one."

I did my best to keep my expression blank. It was good that he mentioned me but did not point me out. It would allow me to watch and observe, without those in the room seeing who it was that was watching. I could be Jerome's other set of eyes.

I would do what he always said I did best...and that was to use my observational skills.

"I realize that you may not believe what I say but I do hope that you will allow me the opportunity of working to prove it to you," Jerome went on.

"Do you know who killed him?" asked the man nearest him, arms folded, brow furrowed.

"No," Jerome said, shaking his head. "But that is why you are all here, so that I might be able to get to the bottom of this, and we can all return to sleep."

"You are being awfully calm for someone who is speaking about the death of a man on this very train," said another man, further toward the back, the one with the burly shoulders. "How do we know it was not you? And you are simply covering for yourself?"

Murmurs of agreement spread through the room and angry glances shifted toward Jerome.

*How quickly people will shift their loyalty...*I thought. Did anyone know the burly man more than they knew Jerome? Was it his authoritative tone or perhaps his stature that caused people to believe him and accept his challenge of Jerome?

Mrs. Montford moved beside me. I expected she was uncomfortable watching her nephew being scrutinized the way he was.

"How do we know someone is actually dead? Has anyone really looked him over?"

"I was the one who found him," came the rather acidic tone of Mrs. Clarkson, who sat in the booth across from us. "He was dead, I tell you. As dead as a doused ember."

Jerome looked over at her and she glared up at him.

"I can't say that I trust what you're saying..." she snapped. "But I don't suppose we have much choice, now, do we? You were right there after I stumbled upon him, and the first to take charge. Men without the experience that you speak of do not simply jump to action without any reservation. As such, you may very well be who you say you are. I am willing to listen to your plans."

I watched her with newfound respect. As impolite as she had been during the course of our trek, this might have been the first time she had said something tolerable.

"Thank you. I will do my best to honor your trust," Jerome said. "As I said, I do not expect you to believe me without cause. Regardless, we must work together to find the person who has done this. We only have so much time."

"Where is the conductor's body now?" someone else asked.

"It is still in one of the last cars," Jerome said. "We have not yet determined what should be done with the corpse."

"So you have simply left it there?"

"How could you be so disrespectful?"

The concerns and fears flew through the air. Men began to speak over one another, trying desperately to find the way to move forward, to make sense of the mess that we found ourselves in.

"Gentlemen, ladies, please..." Jerome said, as there were a few select women in the room, Mrs. Montford and I included, though we had remained silent. He turned to some of the staff that lingered near the door. "Is every compartment accounted for here?"

The uniformed young man, who I had seen running back and forth through the hall near Mr. Bedeau's body, nodded. "Indeed, sir. All have been inspected and spoken to – well, all except for – "

"How is it that this has happened?" asked one of the other women in the car, frowning up at Jerome, clutching her handbag close to her chest as she huddled near the wall. "How did he die?" she asked.

"There is very little that we know right now but my assumption would be that it was perhaps a blow to the back of the head," Jerome said.

"There were no wounds?" asked another.

"We do not have a doctor on board to examine the body but there were no marks that I could see, no," Jerome said. "Which might help us, it might not."

"Why would it not?"

"Because it means that we cannot narrow down what it was that was used to kill him," Jerome said. "It might have been anything heavy."

He looked around the cabin.

"I am going to need any sort of information that anyone aboard this train has to come forward and share. That would help us a great deal and would allow us to figure this out as soon as possible. As such...and I fear that I may regret asking, but does anyone have any information about the conductor they would be willing to share? No information is too small and it could prove useful."

I heard only the sound of my own blood pumping in my ears as I looked around the room. Not a single person raised their hand. Not one.

Either no one knew anything that could help...or they were simply hiding anything they did know.

I looked over at Mrs. Montford, sighing as I pressed my lips tightly together. *I wish this could have gone differently,* I thought. *If only some of the passengers would be willing to speak.*

"No one wants to be accused..." Mrs. Montford whispered to me.

I leaned closer. "That certainly does seem to make sense," I whispered back. "People will do anything to protect themselves."

My eyes swept over the crowd and I saw many wore the same, hardened expressions, which made it difficult to try and discern if any of them could have been the one to kill Mr. Bedeau.

"This is entirely different than any crime we have had to deal with before," I murmured to her.

"What will we do when the train arrives at the station tomorrow?" she asked.

"I do not know," I said. "If we do not find the killer, then it is entirely possible they will flee the train before the police arrive at the station to detain them."

"Which means they need only bide their time for a few more hours," she whispered.

"Yes, that's right," I said.

"Anyone?" Jerome asked, staring out over the crowded dining car. The only sound he received in response was the rumble of the train cars, drawing ever nearer to our destination.

The door behind us was wrenched open and the man in the silk pajamas was ushered through, followed closely by one of the members of the train crew.

"I can make it the rest of the way, sir, *thank you*," he said in a chastising tone, glaring at the crew member over his shoulder.

The uniformed crewman glared back at him, his frown almost entirely hidden behind his thick, ginger beard. "Mr. Townson requested everyone, from every car. You are not an exception, not when there is a murderer on the loose."

"That is *precisely* what I was trying to explain to you – "

He walked around Jerome and stood before him, his hands balled at his sides, his eyes like sharpened daggers.

Jerome watched him coolly. "Yes? Can I help you, Mister..."

"Mr. Dubois, thank you," the man said, lifting his chin with indignation. "I am *appalled* at this whole affair. Dragging people from their compartments to question and interrogate them, instead of protecting them from whoever is responsible? Would it not be wise to instead leave them where they were and go and speak with each family individually?"

Jerome frowned at him. "This is a situation that must be dealt with swiftly. If everyone is here, where I am able to see and speak with them, then I may very well have a chance to discern the truth. They will not be able to run away."

"But they can hide all the better in a room this size," Mr. Dubois said with a sweeping motion, turning to look at the group in the room behind him. "Think of it. The killer is very likely in this room but he is not going to give up useful information in this environment. And everyone's stories of anything they might have seen will be tainted by having heard the stories of others first."

He made a good point and appeared to know it. He must have been used to giving orders the way he was. Wherever he was from, his name must have carried weight, and as such, he found little reason not to stand up to Jerome.

Jerome, however, folded his arms and looked past him at the others in the dining room.

"You are expecting us all to leave our compartments, our families, and our belongings, to come out here and...what? How can you be certain that the killer is not out somewhere right now, entirely ignoring your wishes, preparing to strike again!"

Jerome swallowed, his jaw clenching.

"You have no business ordering us about the way you are," Mr. Dubois said.

"You are correct," Jerome said suddenly.

Startled, I blinked up at him. I had expected him to challenge Mr. Dubois but he relented...and I could not be entirely sure why.

Jerome said, "I realize that my request to bring everyone here was perhaps a bit hasty. I shall simply attribute that to unclear thinking due to the unusual hour. I believe it is a reason why many of us are as fearful and as upset as we are."

I noticed the man with the large shoulders glare, his frown deepening.

"This does not change the urgency of our current predicament," Jerome said. "And while I do believe that being together is a better form of protection, I cannot ask you all to remain separated from your families in this manner. I shall ask members of the staff to station themselves in each car of the train, as well as asking that some of you gentlemen offer to stand guard outside as well. This will hopefully deter the killer from pursuing any further targets."

One of the men nearer the front cleared his throat.

"Yes, sir?" Jerome asked.

"What if it was one of the members of the crew?" he asked.

Jerome nodded. "It very well might have been. My partner has wisely pointed out the fact to me that whoever it was that killed Mr. Bedeau likely had a prior relationship with him."

The suspicious glances then passed between the passengers, each of them looking at the other as if they were staring the killer in the face.

"Yes...why else would they kill him?" Mr. Dubois said, puffing out his chest. "Now, are we free to go back to our rooms?" he asked.

"Yes," Jerome said. "If I have any further questions, I may come to speak with you."

"This was an utter waste of time..." growled the broad-shouldered man, slamming his palms on the table, slowly getting to his feet. "You roused us all, rounded us up as if you had the authority to do so, and for what reason? To tell us all that the conductor is dead and that you do not know who is responsible?"

Jerome cleared his throat. "I have asked that someone volunteer information. There may be someone here who is simply withholding what they know."

"You might as well just tell us the truth..." came a scathing tone from one of the other men, who had risen and now followed the other, bigger man out. "You do not know at all what you are doing."

"I am doing all I can, sir," Jerome said.

The two men walked out but I did not see anyone else move.

"I still trust you," said one man near the front, wearing a green nightcap.

"Thank you," Jerome said. "Now, there really is no one

here who can give me any information that I might be able to go on? Nothing at all?"

The man in the green nightcap shook his head.

"Very well, then. If we can all agree to be available for questions," Jerome said.

"Yes, of course," said one.

"It is not as if I shall be able to sleep at all for the rest of the night," said another.

It took a few moments for the majority of the people to clear out. Only six passengers decided to remain.

"I will not enter my quarters again," said Mrs. Clarkson. "Not while I am staying alone. I shall remain here, in sight of the staff and other passengers."

"I shall return soon, then," Jerome said.

Then he came back to the table where Mrs. Montford and I sat, and slipped into the bench seat across from us.

"You did well, dear," Mrs. Montford said. "As well as you could, given these strange circumstances."

He rubbed his eyes with the flat heel of his palm. "Oh, Aunt Bea, you are being far too kind," he said, pulling his hands away and blinking his red-rimmed eyes. "I made an utter fool of myself by allowing my panic to make decisions for me."

"At the time, it seemed an ideal solution," I said. "Remove everyone from the situation, and as you said, there is safety in everyone being together. I think you were trying to make the best of a difficult situation. These are tight quarters, there was no evidence, and we have limited time."

"Limited time..." Jerome repeated. "I had not even considered – we arrive at the station tomorrow morning. The killer might disembark and disappear from that point. If we are to prevent it, we have to solve this tonight. We do not have a choice."

I nodded in agreement. "Yes, I think we must."

"But where will we begin..." he said, searching my face.

"I believe we should start where you have just mentioned," I said. "With those that knew Mr. Bedeau. Those who had a prior relationship with him."

His eyes widened. "The engineer. You mentioned seeing him just after seeing Mr. Bedeau, yes?"

I nodded again. "Precisely. I think he might be able to shed some light onto all this for us."

"I assume he knows..." Jerome said. "Oh, what am I thinking...if he is the one responsible, of course he would know. Anna, come with me. I think seeing your face might just be what he needs to admit to his nefarious deeds, if he was indeed the one who committed them."

"I will have no part of this," Mrs. Montford said, shaking her head. "You two go on. I...I do not think I can handle all the excitement."

"Of course, dear aunt, I would think our compartment is the best place for you," Jerome said.

Mrs. Montford looked at me, her gaze sharpening.

"You take care of this girl, Jerome," she said. "I will not have it be that she finally has learned the truth of her father, and is on her way to be reunited with him, only to be put into danger once again. Do I make myself clear?"

"You have my word," Jerome said. "I will protect her with my life."

9

Jerome received many sour looks on our walk up toward the front of the train. There were two cars of the more expensive compartments, and the few we were able to see into did not take kindly to his presence.

One woman even rose from her bench, screaming child in her arms, to slam the door of the compartment shut on us as we passed by.

"Tensions are high..." Jerome murmured again, but I could see the worry in the tightness of his jaw as we continued on.

This certainly was the downside of these investigations, was it not? It was easy to make enemies of any who might be accused, especially of those who were entirely innocent. Being looked at as a possible suspect was a terribly unsettling experience. I knew firsthand how destructive it could be for a relationship.

I thought of how I had once suspected Mrs. Montford of a crime and how it had created such distance between us. It amazed me that I had allowed myself to believe it so thoroughly and so easily. Was that why all the passengers had been able to doubt what Jerome had been saying?

It was almost one o'clock in the morning when we reached the front of the train. The noise, the nearly unbearable clacking of the wheels against the rails, and the surge of the smoke from the smokestack, bounced around inside my head, reverberating as if a bell had been struck. A layer of soot covered every surface, which I discovered after following Jerome inside and grasping the handle beside the door to steady myself as we entered the cabin.

"I am sorry to say that we are not even near the engine yet," Jerome said, trying to look out the window. He grimaced as he wiped his sooty hands off on his trousers. The soot had been caked on the windowsill. "The coal car is in front of us and I do not think it wise to traverse that while we are moving."

"How will we see the engineer, then?" I asked.

Jerome frowned, and stared at the door. "You wait here one moment," he said, and disappeared through it.

"Jerome, wait," I said. "You should not be – "

But he was gone.

I sighed, looking around. The sparseness of the car told me that this was a car primarily for the train crew, given the lack of velvet seat cushions and the exposed, steel walls. Some crates filled one corner and a dirty shovel lay up against the wall beside the door.

I rubbed my hands up and down my arms, my teeth beginning to chatter. *Not properly insulated, either,* I thought.

The door slid open a moment later and Jerome returned with a triumphant expression on his face.

"I had one of the boys shoveling coal fetch him," Jerome said. I noticed new streaks of coal on his suit. I set aside the questions I wanted to ask about how they had gotten there.

"And he is coming?" I asked.

"As far as I know, as soon as someone else takes his place for him," Jerome said, glancing over his shoulder. "Perhaps you should step back here a bit. I do not want any unexpected bounce of the track to send you through there, out onto the ground."

*Or perhaps sailing over the side of a bridge...*I thought, my stomach dropping. I took a step back, away from the door.

"What do you think he will say?" I asked, my heart leaping into my throat. "He did seem terribly troubled when he passed by me before the conductor's death."

Jerome's gaze hardened. "He did?" he asked. "That is concerning."

The door slid open a moment later and the engineer appeared. He was shorter than I remembered and a great deal dirtier. He must have been hard at work, keeping the train moving.

Doubts began to plague me. If he was here, working hard –

But he was not so entirely dirty when I last saw him...was he? I wondered.

The man appeared sour, pulling his blackened gloves from his hands, the brightest color from him being the green of his eyes as he stared at me, his dark hair disappearing amidst all the coal dust.

"What is the trouble?" he asked. Even the edges of his lips were coal dusted.

"Good evening," Jerome said. "My name is – "

"I care little for who you are," the man said, his thick brows creasing. "What is so urgent that you needed me to leave my post?"

"It is about Mr. Bedeau," I said. "We have some questions for you."

His eyes narrowed as he regarded me. "One moment..." he murmured. "I recognize you."

"Yes, sir," I said. "Our apologies for interrupting you, but – "

The man furrowed his brow and his green eyes flashed. The worry I had seen in his face earlier had disappeared and instead had been replaced with a deep anger. "Neither of you have permission to be up here," he snapped.

"Our apologies," Jerome said. "My name is Mr. Townson and this is Miss Fairweather. We are looking into the death of Mr. Bedeau."

I noticed that he had wisely left our exact role in this investigation unspoken. If anyone had chosen to challenge our authority, we would have had to admit that we had none, officially.

"What is your name, may I ask?" Jerome asked.

"Mr. Vaux," he said, though reluctant. Some of his anger appeared to change back to worry. I could see the reality of his situation had dawned on him. "I really do not have time to talk. I must keep an eye on the train."

"Mr. Vaux, you do realize that your colleague is dead?" Jerome asked. "That he was killed on this very train?"

"Yes, I know," Mr. Vaux said, and his gaze shifted to the floor. "I was informed just a short while ago. Some of the crew members have already moved his body back to his quarters until we reach our destination."

"That was thoughtful," Jerome said.

"I am certain that you have come here to accuse me of being the one to kill him," Mr. Vaux said, his green eyes flashing again. He reached for the shovel along the wall.

"Mr. Vaux!" Jerome cried, throwing his hands up.

I leapt backward, my heart taking off as if I had heard a gunshot.

"What is the problem?" Mr. Vaux shouted.

"The – the shovel, sir," Jerome said.

Mr. Vaux raised an eyebrow. He lifted the shovel up over his shoulder, a well-practiced, fluid motion. "You're a jumpy pair, aren't you?'"

I gathered myself as best I could, though my cheeks still burned hot. "Mr. Vaux," I said. "What can you tell us of Mr. Bedeau? Of your relationship?"

"Only that I did not kill him. Is that satisfactory?" he asked. "I must get back to the train. It is my responsibility, not that of the fellow I left in charge."

"I can understand that but we need just another moment of your time," I said. "You were the last person I saw this evening, going after Mr. Bedeau to speak with him...which as far as I can see, was not long before he was killed."

He sighed, rubbing his relatively clean hand over his filthy face, leaving streaks. "There is not much to tell," Mr. Vaux said, his tone surprisingly steady. "I was going to speak with him, yes, but it was about one of our boys we had just hired. He gave himself an unpleasant gash with the end of one of the shovels. I knew it best to tell Mr. Bedeau before it got around to him without my intervention."

"It has been said that the two of you argued," I went on. "Even in the afternoon, before the train left, you were arguing."

Mr. Vaux sighed once more. "Yes...Mr. Bedeau and I argued. Perhaps more than we should have. We did not see eye to eye about the workings of the train. He cared more for the passenger's comfort, and I for efficiency. It had always been so, and why we generally stayed out of one another's way. When we worked together, we each agreed to let the other do his own job as he saw fit. Most of the time, that worked..."

He sniffed and then let out an enormous sneeze. He reached into the front of his coveralls and found a sooty handkerchief, which he wiped his dirty nose with.

"I must admit, though...a great deal of the trouble between us was my fault," he said. "I have not been the easiest of men to get along with lately. I...I lost one of my children recently, my youngest...to a terrible sickness."

"I am very sorry to hear that, Mr. Vaux," I said.

He shook his head. "I do not say this to ask for your pity," he said. "I simply say it so you will know why others on the train might have noted that my temper is not the best right now."

Jerome nodded. "Our deepest condolences, Mr. Vaux," he said.

I was surprised Jerome seemed to believe the man's words so easily. His story might simply have been devised to gain our sympathy. Still, I supposed it was wise to allow the engineer to believe that I, too, trusted him.

"I appreciate your kindness," Mr. Vaux said. "I can see quite plainly why someone might have thought I wanted Mr. Bedeau dead. That is far from the truth. I might not have shared his priorities when it came to working on the train, but I did respect his work ethic and the way in which he cared for passengers."

Jerome glanced at me out of the corner of his eye. I could see that he, like me, was trying to decide how far he could believe in the engineer's regret. He must have arrived at the same conclusion I did, that there was nothing to be gained by letting him see our doubts.

"Mr. Vaux, I will not keep you but a moment longer,"

Jerome said. "Having worked with him as you have, is there anyone else that you might know of that might be – "

"Guilty?" Mr. Vaux filled in for him. "I can certainly think of one. And it is rather convenient that she is upon this train this very night."

10

"Who is it that you mean, exactly?" Jerome asked Mr. Vaux.

We stood in the same steel car, with the same *clu-clunk* of the train wheels passing over the tracks beneath us. It seemed an entirely different world, entirely separate from the luxury dining car and plush compartments behind us. In this small, cramped space, there was nothing more than grief and fear, the weight of death pressing in around us.

"I suppose it is possible you might not have seen her, though she is difficult to miss," Mr. Vaux said. "An elderly widow who travels back and forth from England to Venice, a trip that she and her late husband used to take regularly."

"Mrs. Clarkson," I said. "I suspected she might have been who you were speaking of."

Jerome looked at me. "That horrible woman that nearly swatted you with her cane back in Paris?"

I nodded.

"Oh, that would have been tame for her," Mr. Vaux said.

"I have seen her take grown men by the lapels of their coats and give them a shake."

Jerome's brows furrowed. "And you have let her back onto the train?"

"Her husband owned part of one of the railways, if I remember correctly," I said.

"Yes," Mr. Vaux said. "Any further history you should want, you will have to ask her. It is imperative that I return to the engine. We must reach the next station on time."

"Of course," Jerome said. "Thank you for answering our questions."

The engineer tipped his hat and turned toward the door, but paused.

"I wonder what will happen when we reach our destination," he said. "We have never had a crime of this sort since I have worked this line."

Jerome shrugged. "The local authorities will have to be summoned," he said. "It will be difficult, given the deceased was a native of France and we will be in Italy..."

"I know a few officers that frequent the station," Mr. Vaux said. "I shall report the death to them and then the matter will be out of our hands."

"That will be a great relief," I said.

He nodded, and pulled open the door to step out into the rushing wind as it passed over the coal car in front of us.

Jerome huffed as the door closed, and he looked over at me. "The woman he spoke of...is that not the same woman who found the dead body and screamed, waking us all?"

"I believe it is," I said. "Which, now that I think of it, might have been a very clever cover for the deed she had just committed. It would ensure no witnesses and hardly any suspicion, as people quite obviously would have been far more concerned about the body itself than the person who had discovered it."

"Yes..." Jerome said. "It is hard to imagine a woman of her age and stature killing a strong, healthy man, unless she had an accomplice. But if we overlook that for a moment, it is all too easy to suspect her, simply because of her disagreeable demeanor."

I shook my head. "I suppose that had not crossed my mind, though you are right. Mr. Bedeau spoke of her too, remember? He told us how the two of them did not get on well at all. Or rather, that she had issue with him, it seemed."

I looked up at him, worried.

"I must admit that I, too, have trouble imagining a woman as old and frail as she is being strong enough to kill a much younger man," I said. "But as of this moment, she certainly does seem to be a possible suspect, doesn't she?"

"As of this moment, yes," Jerome said.

He reached into the front pocket of his coat and withdrew his pocket watch, flipping it open. "Oh, blast it...this soot is everywhere. I fear I shall never be rid of it..." He squinted at the clock face in the dark. "It's half past one. When are we supposed to arrive at the next station?"

"In about seven and a half hours," I said, my face flushing with renewed anxiety. "Good heavens...how are we to solve this in such short time?"

"I do not know," Jerome murmured. "Let us hope that Mrs. Clarkson will be able to tell us more than what we already know and perhaps guide us down the right path."

"If not being the very answer we are looking for in and of herself," I said.

"Too true," Jerome said. "Shall we, then?"

"Wait," I said, holding my hand up.

Our voices were soft, despite being the only two in the car. I had not noticed until now how very alone we were.

I stared up at him, and when his eyes met mine, it was akin to a key finding its unique lock, sliding home with ease and familiarity. His gaze softened, and for a moment, I searched the clear, blue-green of them.

I love him.

The thought struck me hard. As soon as it passed through my mind, across the path of my conscious thinking, I knew that it was true. Even more so, it was something I had known for quite some time. Weeks. Perhaps months. I had known it, felt it, *chosen* it...yet was only now allowing myself to say the exact words with my own internal voice. My heart became suddenly full, even as all the doubt, fear, and concerns I had about our present situation dissipated. In a way, I suddenly felt...free.

"Anna...?"

With a jolt, I realized that he had spoken to me, and like a fool, all I had done was gaze up at him like a lovesick schoolgirl.

"Oh – yes, I'm sorry," I said, my face burning.

"It's all right," he said, with a chuckle. "It simply seemed as if you lost your train of thought."

"Yes, my train of thought..." I said.

"I realize that it is late," Jerome said. "You must be exhausted."

"No," I said, shaking my head. "I am used to losing sleep. These past few months have been difficult enough, and I do not seem to sleep well when I am so terribly worried – "

I bit down on the inside of my lip.

"What I mean to say, is that I – I was considering...oh, what was I considering?" I said.

I forced the newly discovered thoughts from my mind. It

was not the time, nor the place, to be swooning over Jerome. How could I even *think* of such things at a time like this?

"I believe you wanted to say something about Mrs. Clarkson?" he asked.

"Mrs. Clarkson…" I repeated. "Yes, I believe that I should be the one to speak with her."

"Really?" Jerome asked. He pursed his lips, considering. "Well, it might be more advantageous, I suppose. I wonder if she will give us the chance."

"We will only know if we ask, yes?" I asked. "If I remember rightly, she decided to stay back in the dining car."

"She may very well still be there," he said. "I believe we saw her when we passed through."

"Very good," I said. I gathered my courage and looked up at him. "Shall we, then?"

We started back through the car and my heart sank a bit as we left that car, as if I was leaving a momentous moment behind, forever trapped within those walls. Why could I not have realized the depth of my affections for Jerome in a more romantic setting, instead of one covered in a thin layer of soot?

The dining car had emptied further, leaving only three patrons sitting at tables as far away from one another as they could. In the bench closest to us, one man had stretched out and fallen asleep, snoring beneath the table. Another woman, who could hardly have been older than I, sat at one of the booths partway down the car, staring out the window. The plate before her remained untouched, as did the cup of coffee rippling softly with each bump of the wheels over the tracks.

Mrs. Clarkson, too, had remained in the dining car as she had said she would, seated at the booth far on the opposite side. She had not seen us enter the car, as she seemed engrossed in the cross-stitch in her small, boney hands. It seemed she had at least gone back to her compartment for something to occupy herself with.

I paused, turning to Jerome. "Perhaps you should stay here and observe?" I murmured. "That way she does not think you are eavesdropping?"

"She will surely see me sitting here," he said. "And if you tell her who you are..."

I frowned. He was right, of course. There was likely no getting around it. It would probably not be wise to lie to her about anything.

"Very well. But allow me the chance to speak with her out of earshot," I said. "Perhaps she would be willing to say more if she knows that you are not immediately involved in the conversation."

He nodded. "Agreed. I shall remain here, unless you need me."

"I shall wave you over if I do," I said.

I turned and started toward her, my heart beginning to race once more. Dread seeped into my bones as I approached her, waiting for her to look up and see me.

When she did, it was as if her gaze alone had struck me with daggers of ice. She did not slow her progress on her stitching, however, continuing on to make what I imagined might be the branch of some sort of fruit tree. "You again," she spat, grimacing up at me. "What do you want? Come to bother a poor old woman?"

"No, ma'am, not at all," I said. "May I join you?" I asked, gesturing to the empty booth across from her.

"Absolutely not," she said, her gaze darting up to me, her eyes like narrow slits. It did not at all match the ease with which she passed the needle up, over, and under the linen. "What do you want?"

The blush returned to my face. It had begun worse than I might have hoped. "My name is Anna Fairweather and I am investigating the death of the conductor."

The woman burst into laughter, the wrinkles in her old face deepening as she did so. "You?" she asked, chuckling a moment more. "That is quite a laugh, isn't it?"

"I realize you might think I am joking, madam, but I assure you, I am assisting Mr. Townson," I said, trying to muster a tone of authority. Sadly, I thought I sounded more like a child trying to act older than it was.

Mrs. Clarkson barked another laugh. "I must thank you, dear. I have not laughed that hard in some time. If you want, you can sit with me...until this whole ridiculous affair passes and that lanky, rather plain looking young man who also seems to be playing detective realizes that the conductor had a heart attack and died naturally."

I stared at her, gently easing myself into the seat across from her. "You think he simply...died?"

She rolled her eyes. "Well, of course. The idea that he was murdered is absurd. There would have been more to prove that theory, yes? A wound of some sort, a sound that would have alerted us all before I found him lying there on the floor."

I thought back to the fear that had been plain on her face right after she had found him, when I had first seen the horrific scene. The words she spoke now certainly did not match to what she had been feeling then. Her body language had betrayed her, but I chose to keep that thought to myself.

"I take it you could not sleep and that is why you stepped out of your compartment when you did?" I asked. I could see that my best course of action to ask her the questions I wanted answered would be to do my best to not let her know I was searching for information. I would need to tread carefully and simply ask questions that were only in relation to what she was spouting off. If I could keep her talking...

"Yes," she said, simply. "It is not as if I sleep a great deal anymore as it is. When you get old, you will feel very fortunate if you are able to get a few hours at a time. Far too often, you simply lie there and think..."

She glared across at me. "Why are you awake at this hour?"

"I...I could not sleep after what happened earlier," I said.

Her eyes narrowed, her bottom lip protruding slightly. "It amazes me that anyone can sleep. You might yet have more sense than you appear to, girl," she said.

"Why do you say that?" I asked. "That it amazes you that anyone can sleep?"

She snickered. "Perhaps I was wrong about you, after all. It is easy to be mistaken. My son continues to tell me that my faculties are slipping. A man is dead, girl. Dead! Died right outside of the room where people are sleeping, sitting, laughing, talking – as dead as can be!"

"I am surprised, madam, how easily you can speak of a man's death," I said. "Everyone I have spoken with tonight cannot seem to utter a word about it, as terrified as they are."

"When you are as old as I, then you will have seen more death than any person should have to," she said. "Though I would not expect someone like you to understand."

"You would be very surprised, I think," I murmured.

The words had left my lips before I had even realized they had formed in my mind. In my great annoyance with the woman, in my frustration at her belittling of me, I decided to try and show her up.

Her eyes flashed and her jaw clenched. "You dare make light of what I have endured?" she sneered. "You have *no* idea what I have lived through, what I have seen with my own two eyes…"

She set down her cross stitch, and my heart skipped. What was she going to do?

A server approached our table then, his eyes wide, a nervous smile plastered to his face. "Good evening, ladies. Might I interest you in – "

"A coffee," the old woman snapped. "And if it does not come with a tart with the proper amount of cream atop it, the chef shall hear from me again."

The server looked over at me, raising his brows. I realized that he had come over with the intention of checking in on me. He must have heard Mrs. Clarkson's raised voice. Perhaps he wanted to intercede?

"Is there anything I can get for you, miss?" he asked.

"She will have nothing," Mrs. Clarkson hissed, her eyes slits as she glared at me.

I hesitated, and as much as I despised having to endure this sort of treatment, I swallowed my pride and assumed the dutiful role of servant. *Mrs. Montford would never treat me this way…*I thought. *But my work has certainly taught me how to hold my tongue in someone's presence.* "Thank you, but I was just stopping here for a moment. Perhaps when I rejoin my companion, I shall – "

"I thought I asked you to bring me some *coffee!*" she snapped. "Now!"

The server gave me an apologetic frown and then hurried off.

I did my best not to be intimidated by this woman, who

cared little for anyone who might oppose her.

Her eyes fixed upon me once more and the dislike only deepened in her expression. "You will not understand what true pain is until you have to watch your own husband die right before your very eyes," she hissed at me over the table, not bothering to keep her voice down, though there were few left in the dining car to hear. "To watch someone fade away, to see the very life drain from them…"

"What happened to him?" I asked. "How did he – "

"Die?" Mrs. Clarkson asked, as if forcing herself to say the word with as much force as possible, as though she found it somehow cathartic. "Stabbed to death, by one of the cooks who thought he complained too much. I found out later that the cook, who had been hired only six months prior, was a known criminal that had taken the job at our estate as a means of hiding from the authorities. It was all because of one error, one simple mistake, that my husband was killed. There was nothing I could do about it."

Suddenly, I understood. Everything about her made sense.

"Did this happen recently?" I asked.

"No," she said, sourly. "Nearly ten years ago. The anniversary is in three days."

That would certainly explain her high levels of hostility, not only toward me but toward everyone.

"I suppose you might say that you have become rather numb to death, then," I said. "Mr. Bedeau's death does not affect you the same way that it might have affected – "

"I cared little for the man when he was alive," she hissed.

"Did you know him well?" I asked.

"Hardly," she said. "My husband owned part of this railway, and as such, he and I were free to take trips all throughout Europe whenever we wanted. An annual tradition we had was to leave from Paris and travel to Venice as spring drew near to enjoy the milder weather. That is what this trip is for me."

"You still make the journey, even without your husband?"

"You are *daft,* girl," she said. "I am here, am I not? Yes, I still make this journey."

"And Mr. Bedeau was the conductor on this rail?" I asked. "That is how you knew him?"

"I did not know him," she said. "I disliked him the moment I saw him. The man was entirely dishonest. When he smiled, it was nothing more than a lie. He was putting on an act and I could not stand it."

"An act?" I asked. "You did not think him to be genuine?"

"Of course not," she said. "I could see right through his schemes. All he ever wanted was a hefty tip, and more than that, he wanted to be promoted to some place higher in the company, thinking the role of conductor to be beneath him."

"Really?" I asked. "Well, that certainly does not seem so terrible, does it? What harm is there in someone wanting to make more of themselves?"

"That is not the *point*," she hissed. She grimaced and shook her head. "His...expressions, the way he spoke...every part of him, it simply – it grated upon me."

I drew in a small gasp. "He reminded you of the man who killed your husband..." I murmured.

An explosion of anger bloomed behind her eyes. "You..." she hissed. "You do not know what you speak of!"

My heart began to race. Perhaps this was it! Perhaps I had found the truth! If she killed Mr. Bedeau, then this would be more than believable motive, would it not?

The server appeared at that moment, and set the

steaming cup of coffee down before her, along with a charming fruit tart with a heart dollop of clotted cream. He laid an olive green napkin down beside her plate, likely wanting to avoid the hand slap of laying it across her lap himself. "Here you are, madam," he said, giving her a worried smile, as if politely asking her to spare him her wrath.

Without a word further, he scurried away.

She snatched the spoon, and without mercy, slashed it through the tart. The cream collapsed beneath the strike and melded with the dripping fruit of the berries and apricot jam. She brought the spoon to her mouth, heaped with the tart, and chomped down on it much like a young child would.

If her husband had been killed by the cook and Mr. Bedeau unknowingly reminded her of the murderer...

She snatched the cloth from the table and brought it to her mouth, wiping away the excess cream.

As she set it back down, I noticed a smudge of white that was not at all from the cream. It was a powder of some sort that had come from the palms of her hands.

"What are you staring at?" Mrs. Clarkson snapped, drawing the napkin back beneath the table, out of my sight.

"Your hand..." I said. "Are you wearing some sort of powder?"

To my surprise, her face flushed scarlet. "I am, if you *must* know," she said, sitting up straighter. "Talcum powder. My hands have been so terribly dry in this cold weather. Talcum powder is the only thing that seems to help with the cracking." She rubbed her hands together and I could see some of the powder had not been properly rubbed into the backs of her hands. It slowly disappeared and she resumed eating her tart.

That powder might be useful, I thought. *If she uses it, and if she killed Mr. Bedeau, it is very likely that traces of it could be on his body or at the scene of the murder...*

"What are you still doing here?" the old woman asked, glowering at me. "You have no business lingering."

"My apologies, madam," I said, sliding out of the booth and straightening up. "I thought that you still wanted the company."

"Not from the likes of you," she spat. "Trying to tell me why I disliked Mr. Bedeau, trying to tell me that you have lived more than I, experienced more terrible things than I have – "

She smacked the table.

"Server! Bring me another tart!"

"Have a pleasant evening, madam," I said, dipping into a low curtsy and turning away.

The smile slipped off my face as soon as I started back down through the dining car toward Jerome.

He set down the newspaper that he had been pretending to read, his eyes wide with expectant nervousness. "I only heard bits of it," he said. "What did you – "

"Come along," I said in a low voice. I waved him to follow me, and he came after me.

Mrs. Clarkson did not even look up at us as we passed by her. I was not at all upset over that fact.

As soon as we were out in the narrow hall between the dining car and the exterior platforms leading back to the day car, I rounded on him. "I have my doubts but it is entirely possible that it was Mrs. Clarkson."

"Really?" Jerome asked. "How do you know?"

"There is only one way to know for certain..." I said. "We need to see Mr. Bedeau's body."

11

"Talcum powder?" Jerome repeated as we made our way through the second to last compartment car, on our way back to the last car where the private quarters of the train crew resided. It was the place where we were informed Mr. Bedeau's body had been laid for the rest of our journey. "Why talcum powder?"

"It is to help with moisture," I said. "Women use it for their skin, and she would not be the first older woman I have known to choose it as a means of maintaining as much of her youth as possible. It is often used for infants, as well, as a prevention for diaper rash."

Jerome nodded. "Yes, I know. But how did the conversation come up?"

"I saw it, smudged on the napkin from her hands," I said. "If it brushed off so easily onto the napkin, then there is a very good chance it would show up on Mr. Bedeau's dark grey suit somewhere, somehow."

Jerome frowned. "I do not remember seeing anything of the sort on the man," he said. "Though I suppose that could be because I was not looking for it."

"I was just about to say that," I said. "How could we have known? And would you have even suspected anything if you had seen it?"

"In the moving of his body, it is possible that it could have rubbed off by now," Jerome said.

"I know," I said. "Which is why we must inspect it very carefully."

My nerves hummed a bit as we passed from one car to the next. A great deal of the charm of overnight trains had been lost on me during this journey. I did not know if I would ever want to take another trip quite like this for some time.

I worried what we might find on Mr. Bedeau. I knew full well that this small detail might very well not be enough to go on. If we found nothing, I was not entirely sure in what direction we would move next.

We entered the last car. At once, we were greeted by one of the young men dressed in the same uniform as Mr. Vaux. He stepped between us and the short hall that lay beyond. "My apologies but this car is for the crew only. You will have to return to your compartments."

"We are here to look at the body of Mr. Bedeau," Jerome said. "My name is Mr. Jerome Townson and this is Miss Fairweather. We are working to help with the death of Mr. Bedeau."

The young man's brow furrowed and he glanced back and forth between the two of us. "I thought I recognized you," he said. "But Mr. Vaux said that we are not allowed to let anyone in here."

"What is your name?" I asked, trying a friendlier tone.

"Jacques," said the young man. "Jacques Farrow."

"Well, Mr. Farrow, you have done your job well," I said. "I assume that no one else has been back here to see him?"

He shook his head. "No, ma'am."

I looked at Jerome. "That is good news. Hopefully it means no one will have tampered with the body."

"Precisely," he said. "Young man, I appreciate your refusal to abandon your duties, but it is very important that we have a chance to look at the body. The train will be arriving at the next station in – "

"In less than six hours, sir," the young man said, answering for Jerome.

"Yes," Jerome said. "Six hours. Then it is even more imperative that you allow us to see him. If you had any liking for the conductor at all, I am sure you would want us to find the person responsible for his death."

Mr. Farrow looked over his shoulder, glancing toward the first door to his left. "I...I have not been able to look at him since – since – "

"You do not need to worry," I said. "We will take care of it for you."

The youth nodded and stepped aside. "All I ask is that you treat him with respect," he murmured. "Mr. Bedeau was always kind to me. I – I looked up to him."

"We will do our very best, I assure you," I said.

I walked around him at the same time that Jerome clapped the boy on the shoulder. I waited beside the door and allowed him to push it open.

Inside the small room was a humble living arrangement. I noticed a small desk, a plain, wooden chair, and a trunk at the foot of an iron-framed bed.

Lying in that bed, draped in a simple linen blanket as if we had caught him in the middle of a nap, was Mr. Bedeau.

My heart began to race. I had not done many examinations of corpses.

"You have usually been the one to do this," I muttered to

Jerome as he closed the door behind us. "Looking over the victims, that is."

"Would you wish to wait out in the hall?" he asked. "It would be no trouble."

"Surely you cannot be so eager or so indifferent..." I said under my breath, knowing full well the young man we had just encouraged stood on the other side of the door. There was no telling if he was leaning against the door, perhaps listening in.

"I certainly would not say eager..." Jerome said. "It is hard to explain. It is not as if they have become easier to look at. It is still a person, after all. A person we were speaking to not more than a few hours ago, no less. It is difficult to stomach."

My face colored. "I apologize for assuming it is easy for you."

"No, no, you need not," he said, shaking his head. "It has simply fallen to me. Someone must take the hard tasks, yes? Anyway...we might as well get started," he said, taking a step toward the cot.

He slowly pulled back the blanket.

"Now that I look more closely, there does seem to be some bruising here, along the hairline..." he said.

I leaned forward. I could see the purple blooming just above the dead man's brow. "That is a rather large bruise," I said, my heart sinking. "The size of a fist. Perhaps even larger."

"Yes," Jerome said, scratching his chin. "Apart from his lantern, there was nothing in the hall that could have been used as a weapon."

"Which would lead me to believe that whoever did this likely hid the weapon," I said.

"Or perhaps used something unexpected as a weapon,

something that we might not even notice in the first place..."
he said.

He stood there in silence, simply staring down at the
body.

Lost in thought, I knew.

I took the chance to look down at Mr. Bedeau's suit.

Mrs. Clarkson was a small woman, rather short,
hunched over with a cane. If she had attacked Mr. Bedeau,
then it was likely that the talcum powder would have
rubbed off in a place where she might have been able to
reach, such as his arm or the front of his coat.

I pulled the blanket back further and hesitated.

I had only ever touched a dead body one other time. I
had held her, in fact, that woman in Brighton. I had not
known that she was dead until after I had helped drag her
ashore. It had been traumatizing, to say the least. That poor
woman's death had stuck with me and her face was one that
I saw more than the others in my nightmares.

Now it seemed I would have to swallow my fear and do
some proper investigating.

*It is only clothing...*I thought.

I leaned in closer to the sleeve, examining it. The dark
grey of the wool blend would have held onto the fine
powder better than even the linen napkin Mrs. Clarkson
had used in the dining car, yet I did not see the faintest
mark. No smudge, no smear. Something should have been
evident.

"Jerome, can you lift his other arm?" I asked.

Jerome nodded but the tightness in his jaw told me he
was about as thrilled about touching the body as I was.

I stared at the other sleeve. "Nothing," I said. "I see no
powder."

I checked the front of the coat as well, thinking she

might have perhaps grabbed onto his lapel to give him a good shake...but once again, I saw nothing.

"There would surely be some of the talcum powder pressed into his coat," I said. "It is so fine that it would simply not be possible for anyone to brush it all away."

"Yes, I thought so as well," Jerome said. "And I do not see any."

"Nor I," I said. "There is certainly some dirt here on the front of his coat but as he was lying on the floor of the car..."

I pushed aside the sadness, the disgust...I needed to keep my mind as clear and calm as I could at the moment, lest I allow my fear to take over and I would no longer be of any help to Jerome.

"Then do you suppose that Mrs. Clarkson is innocent?" he asked.

"I don't know," I said. "The talcum powder seemed to be such a strong possibility. I had really hoped it would give us an obvious answer."

"Did she say anything suspicious when you spoke with her?" Jerome asked.

"Yes. Mrs. Clarkson rather despised Mr. Bedeau because he reminded her of the man who killed her husband," I said. "That being said, she is disagreeable with everyone. When I pointed out that her dislike of Mr. Bedeau may very well have been misplaced, she became quite flustered, as if she were...embarrassed."

Jerome considered, pursing his lips. "Do you suppose she had never made the connection before?"

"I do not know," I said. "Regardless, Mr. Bedeau may have reminded her of the man that killed her husband but he was not the man that did so. Besides, the husband's death happened years ago. Her anger would be far removed."

"I have heard of people killing for less," Jerome said,

frowning. "Grief can do terrible things to a person, especially if they are left to dwell on it all on their own."

"All too true..." I said. "I am glad that your aunt has you to help her through losing her husband."

Jerome gave me a sidelong glance. "What do you mean? You are clearly the support she has needed in this time."

I swallowed, uncertain how to answer.

Jerome, thankfully, seemed to understand that I did not know how, and he pulled the blanket back up to Mr. Bedeau's chin.

"I must admit, Anna, I am rather worried..." Jerome said. "If we do not find the killer before we arrive in Italy, then it is likely he or she will be able to get away with it. There are simply not enough crew members to keep all the passengers aboard. By the time we are able to summon the police...Not only that, but we will have to deal with the differences in both language and law, and determine where precisely he died, whether it was in France or in Italy..."

He shook his head, rubbing his temple.

"It is simply a mess."

"It certainly is," I said. I looked back over at Mr. Bedeau. "We have no further clues, then?"

Jerome shook his head. "And neither of the two people we have suspected have any evidence against them. At least, as far as we know." He huffed. "It is frustrating not to know who it could have been."

"No one has been willing to provide us with much information," I said. "And the body does not seem to be giving us any further clues."

Jerome wrinkled his nose. "I am finding it difficult to think in here. Why don't we step out, and perhaps return to – "

He stopped, blinked a few times, and looked over at me.

"Perhaps we have more information than I thought," he said. "Anna, there certainly is someone else who has been behaving strangely, especially compared to the rest of the passengers on the train!"

I thought for a moment, my brow furrowing. "Well, there has been a great deal of fear, which only makes sense," I said. "Families with children are worried and angry, the fathers and husbands simply wanting their wives and children to be left alone..."

Then it struck me and I looked up at him with wide eyes.

"That businessman," I said. "The one who was arguing with the crew."

Jerome nodded. "Yes, precisely," he said, an excited smile spreading across his handsome face. "He was resistant to leaving his compartment, was he not?"

My heart skipped. "And is his compartment not the one at the very end?"

"Right where Mr. Bedeau's body was lying when it was found?" Jerome asked.

My heart thundered in my ears. An overwhelming urge to kiss Jerome washed over me...dampened only by the fact that there was a dead body in the room with us.

"Let's go speak with him," Jerome said. "And find out precisely what he has to hide."

12

J erome and I were stopped by the young man outside the compartment.

"I hope you were able to find what you were looking for," he said, his eyes eagerly searching my face in particular.

"It gave us some of the answers we were seeking, yes," I said, careful to choose my words in a way that would not be a lie but would not give him false hope. "We are hoping that we are closer to the truth."

He visibly relaxed, his shoulders sagging and a weak smile appearing on his tired face. *He looks as if he has aged ten years overnight...*I thought.

"I shall not keep you from your investigating," he said. "You can trust me to protect Mr. Bedeau. No one will come back here who is not meant to."

"If I were you, I would ensure that *no one* comes back here. Not even the crew. Who is to say that it is not one of them?" I asked.

Horror passed over the young man's face, his mouth

hanging open. "Oh, yes, of course," he said. "Why had I not thought of that?"

"It's all right, you are doing a fine job," Jerome said. "We will probably be back soon."

"Of course," he said. "Anything you require, sir, miss, you simply need ask."

"Thank you," I said.

Jerome pulled open the door for us and we slipped out to the last passenger car.

"Perhaps it would be wise to investigate the scene where he died," I said. "I wonder if we missed something."

"I will fetch a lantern from our compartment," Jerome said. "And that will allow me to check in on my aunt. I am certain she will be pacing the floor with worry."

He was correct.

"WHERE HAVE YOU BEEN?" Mrs. Montford asked, dashing to the door when Jerome pulled it open.

"One moment," Jerome said, ushering me inside and closing the door before he said anything further. "My apologies. Some conversations ran a bit longer than we anticipated."

"What have you learned?" she asked.

"Not a great deal," Jerome said with a sigh.

"Well, we may have learned who the killer is *not*," I said. "Which, I suppose, is good in and of itself."

"What about that Mrs. Clarkson?" Mrs. Montford asked.

Jerome shook his head.

"Probably not," I said. "We thought it might have been, but after speaking with her and looking at the body, we have been unable to determine if it was her."

"It seems unlikely," Jerome added. "Given the injury to his head, the victim was struck quite hard. Mrs. Clarkson would probably have been physically unable to cause such damage."

"What if she struck him with her cane?" Mrs. Montford asked.

"The wound is larger than that," I said. "He must have been hit with something bigger and heavier."

Mrs. Montford frowned. "Do you have a new suspect?"

Jerome and I looked at one another. "Possibly," he said. "That angry businessman who refused to accompany the rest of us into the dining car."

Mrs. Montford's eyes widened. "Oh..." she said.

My heart rate quickened. "What is it?"

She rubbed her collarbone, her forehead wrinkling. "There was shouting down the hall a short time ago. Not entirely surprising, as I can hardly believe anyone old enough to understand what has happened tonight is sleeping, but it caused many of us to look outside the compartments to see what the matter was. I, for one, worried that someone else might have been about to meet his end."

"What happened?" I asked.

"That businessman was shouting at one of the crew who had been coming around, trying to take up the tasks that Mr. Bedeau would have typically taken care of. He stopped here, as well, asking if I wanted anything to eat or drink. I thanked him but declined and he went on his way. Well... when he reached the last compartment, where this businessman you mentioned is staying, the man began to shout at the crewman. I peered out, worried about something terrible happening, the way he was carrying on."

She shook her head and her brow furrowed in anger.

"There has to be something in that compartment that he

does not want anyone to see," she said. "I can think of no other reason for becoming so extraordinarily enraged at anyone who dares approach him."

Jerome scratched his cheek. "He did seem awfully put out at being made to join the rest of us in the dining car," he said.

"Yes," I said. "He convinced you to send everyone back to their compartments. If Mrs. Montford is correct, then he would have naturally wanted to protect his belongings."

Jerome's eyes narrowed. "Do you think it is possible he would have killed Mr. Bedeau to keep those belongings safe, whatever they are?"

"What could he be hiding?" I asked.

"Perhaps something valuable," Jerome suggested.

"Such as a stolen item," I said.

Jerome mused aloud. "He was caught with the stolen item. He killed to cover his tracks..." He began to pace back and forth across the narrow space, taking two steps before turning on his heel and proceeding back. "If our unfortunate conductor caught the businessman in something, perhaps something illegal, then that would have made it necessary to silence him."

"You will need to get into the man's compartment," Mrs. Montford said in a steely voice. "And you will have to realize that you will surely be stepping into a dangerous place."

Her eyes shifted to me, and at once, I knew what she was going to ask.

"No," I said. "I am going to go with him."

"You should stay. It is not safe," Mrs. Montford said. "We are so close to finding your father, and – "

"Aunt Bea, I think that she should be free to make the choice for herself," Jerome said.

For a moment, Mrs. Montford and I stared at one another.

For four years, I had grown used to listening to her thoughts, to her requests, and her orders. It was a familiar way of life and I had become quite content with our relationship and the dynamics in it. I never questioned what she asked me to do and never challenged her.

Here, now, however...it seemed that I would be standing up to her, defying her.

Truly, we had come to a crossroads and it seemed that we might not ever be able to go back.

And if I am honest with myself, I do not know if I want to.

"I wish to go with Jerome," I said. "I must see this through."

She studied my face for a long moment. Something flickered in her eyes. An unspoken respect? Slowly, she nodded. When she did, I knew we had reached a new understanding.

"Very well," she said, before becoming brisk and turning her attention to Jerome. "If you do not bring her back in one piece, then it will be your hide that I am after."

"I will protect her with my very life," he said. "You need not worry about me."

Mrs. Montford's eyes flashed. "I know," she said. "I am quite certain that there has never been another woman that you have – "

"We are running out of time," Jerome said, reaching for the door and sliding it open. "We must speak with him, before it is too late."

"Yes, of course," I said, and without another look at Mrs. Montford, slipped out into the hall.

Jerome came out with me and closed the door behind

himself. "She is fond of you, you know," he said. "I know that the way you came into her care is not at all how it should have been but I think she is going to do all she can to change that."

"I...There is a great deal to think about, isn't there?" I asked. I shook my head. "Not now, though. We must take great care, Jerome. I am worried that this man is worked up enough that he might attack anyone who approaches his door."

"You are correct," Jerome said. "And he will very likely become hostile when he sees that it is the two of us who have come to call."

Fear surged through my veins, numbing the tips of my fingers, making the pounding in my ears grow louder with each step I took.

Jerome stopped just before we reached the compartment door and glanced down at the floor...where Mr. Bedeau had been lying just a few hours before.

"Shall we inspect it closer?" I asked.

Jerome frowned. "I do not know what truths it might reveal to us, if any," he said. "First, I think it would be best for us to speak to the suspect." He turned and looked at me over his shoulder. "Though I cannot for the life of me remember his name, can you?"

I pursed my lips. "I believe...Mr. Du...Mr. Du...bois?"

"Mr. Dubois," Jerome nodded. "I think you are correct."

He straightened his shoulders and approached the door.

Jerome knocked on the wooden frame of the door, and a moment later, we heard rustling from inside. "Who is it?" came a heated demand.

"Is this the compartment of Mr. Dubois?" Jerome asked.

More rustling. "Yes – Yes it is," said the voice. "What do you want?"

"I was hoping to ask you a few questions, Mr. Dubois," Jerome said. It amazed me how steady his voice was. "If you would give me the chance."

A shape appeared behind the opaque glass and the door slid open.

Mr. Dubois glared out into the hall at us, his mouth turned down in an impatient frown. "What could you possibly want from me?" he asked.

"As I said, I had some questions to ask you...about Mr. Bedeau," Jerome said.

I peered over Mr. Dubois' shoulder into his compartment. It was an utter mess inside. Clothes were strewn over every surface. Crumpled papers littered the floor. A map lay stretched out over his bunk, with large, red circles drawn on seemingly random areas. Upon a closer look, it was a map of an unfamiliar city, but the waterways that filled it made me think, with some certainty, that it was Venice.

Mr. Dubois stepped in front of my view, his brow furrowing. "Who?" he asked, his accent thick. "I do not know of whom you speak."

"The dead conductor," Jerome said, his brow furrowing. "Surely there could not be anyone else of importance that I would want to speak with you about."

Mr. Dubois rolled his eyes. "Very well," he said. "But I can assure you, I know nothing."

"Did you have any former relationship with Mr. Bedeau before his death?" Jerome asked.

"No," Mr. Dubois said at once. "I had never met him."

I watched him closely as he spoke. That statement, at the very least, seemed to be the truth.

"All right," Jerome said. "What were you doing when Mr. Bedeau was found dead?"

"Sleeping," Mr. Dubois said, a bite in his words. "As was everyone else on the train."

"Well, certainly not everyone," Jerome said. "I only ask because the death seemed to occur right outside of your compartment."

"And so that is reason enough to accuse me?" Mr. Dubois asked, prodding himself in the chest. "Bah...you know not of what you speak."

"My apologies, Mr. Dubois, but I have not accused you of anything," Jerome said. "All I am asking is simply – "

"You have no other reason to come here other than to blame the fool man's death on me!" he snapped. "It is nearly four in the morning. Some of us would prefer to get some *sleep* before we arrive at our destination."

My heart began to race. Jerome had been right that he would become hostile. Fury seemed to be brewing just below the surface.

"And you mean to tell me that the death of someone upon this train does not trouble you?" Jerome asked. "That you do not want to help us find who is responsible?"

"I hardly care at all about some stranger I did not know," Mr. Dubois said. "And why should I?"

"Excuse me, sir, but were you not the one who came into the dining car, rather begrudgingly, saying that you desired to return to your compartment out of fear of the murderer running rampant on the train?" I asked.

Jerome glanced sidelong at me, and Mr. Dubois' mouth fell open.

"Well, I *never* – " he said. "I have no obligation to speak with you. I know nothing, I have seen nothing, and I would very much like to return to my privacy. Good night."

He began to yank the compartment door closed as he

turned away but Jerome stuck his foot in the gap, preventing it from shutting.

When Jerome pulled it back open, the man whirled around, his handsome face screwed up in anger. "What are you doing?" he snapped. "This, sir, is trespassing."

I followed Jerome inside, my eyes sweeping the space once more.

"I believe there is something that you are not sharing with us," Jerome said, his voice cool and collected, a stark contrast to the nervous tone of Mr. Dubois. "I believe that you are lying."

I caught a glimpse of a suitcase peeking out from underneath the bench near the man's feet. It lay open. I could only see a small corner of it...

My stomach twisted.

Inside lay stacks of money, all tied in string, and a gold bar that glinted in the warm light of the sconces along the wall.

Mr. Dubois noticed my searching gaze, for he stuck his foot out and shoved the suitcase back beneath the bench.

"Out!" he shouted. He stretched his hands out, grabbed the both of us by our sleeves, and pushed us back through the doorway.

With a slam, he shut the compartment door in our faces.

"Money..." I said under my breath, too startled to fully comprehend what had just happened.

"What?" Jerome asked. "What did you say?"

I turned my face up to his. "Money, Jerome..." I said. "An entire suitcase full! And gold bars! Where could he have – "

"Calm down," Jerome said, worry drawing his brows together. He laid his hands on my shoulders. "It's all right. Are you quite certain?"

I pressed a hand against my now pounding head. "That must be why..." I murmured.

I turned and beat upon the door.

"Mr. Dubois, you cannot hide it," I called through the glass. "I saw the suitcase. I know what you are hiding."

Silence greeted us.

Jerome tried the door. It remained locked.

"I could break it down," he said. "I would prefer not to but if I must..."

"Mr. Dubois," I said, knocking on the door again. "Mr. Dubois, are you listening?"

Still he said nothing.

Jerome's face fell. "You do not suppose he is going to do something rash?"

"It is possible," I said, my own stomach dropping in fear. "He is trapped, after all. There is nowhere to go, nowhere to run..."

I took a hesitant step back, away from the door, the knots in my stomach writhing in fear.

"One moment..." Jerome said. "What if that money is his own? We cannot assume that it is the reason Mr. Bedeau is dead. What if he is simply worried that someone might learn he is traveling with a great deal of money and they might try to rob him?"

"We must ask him," I said. "If that is true, then surely he will tell us."

"Right," Jerome said. He pounded on the door again. "Mr. Dubois, we would like to ask you about the money. We realize that you may very well – "

The door flew open suddenly and Mr. Dubois launched himself out at Jerome. It happened so fast that I barely had time to understand what I was seeing.

Mr. Dubois leapt over the threshold, swinging a metal

bar he must have grabbed from somewhere inside his compartment.

Jerome had no time to react.

I heard the sickening thud of the weapon striking flesh, as Jerome was hit across the temple.

Immediately, he collapsed to the floor and lay still.

13

"Jerome..." I cried, shock and fear stealing the breath from my lungs. I tried to hurry to his motionless form but Mr. Dubois stood blocking me.

"I don't think so," he murmured, his expression one of smug confidence.

I glanced over my shoulder. Mrs. Montford, back in our compartment, was only partway down the car. She would surely hear me if I called –

I gasped as Mr. Dubois suddenly crossed the distance between us to grab hold of the front of my dress, pulling me close so that I would be staring him right dead in the eye.

"You will not scream..." he whispered, his eyes wide and dangerous. "If you try, I will snap your neck before you have the chance to utter a sound."

I looked down at Jerome, sprawled out on the floor. He had not moved since he had fallen.

My heart began to race. I could only see him. With each beat of my frantic heart, I waited for him to stir.

He did not.

I studied his back and saw no movement.

Fear stabbed straight through me. Had I lost him?

"They'll find your bodies along the side of the track someday..." Mr. Dubois said. "It might not be for weeks. It is rather sparse out in these parts. They may only be able to identify you based on reports spread up and down the train line, saying that a couple had fallen from the train. I will tell them that I tried to stop you, that the pair of you were so angry with one another, that he pushed you and then couldn't bear to live himself..."

My throat had grown utterly tight and fear had taken hold of my voice, keeping me silent.

"You should have left well enough alone..." he murmured.

He lifted the metal bar he still gripped in his free hand, but I had anticipated him.

If only he knew how many murderers I had to flee from in the past.

I drew back my foot and kicked him in the knee, using every bit of force I could muster.

His leg buckled and he released me for just an instant while he steadied himself.

That was all the time I needed. I leapt backward and turned to run. I had to put distance between myself and Mr. Dubois.

"Help!" I shouted. "Mr. Dubois is after me! He killed Mr. Bedeau!"

I tore open the door out to the next sleeping car, and had just about managed to shut it tight before Mr. Dubois reached it, close on my heels.

I held my breath and hurried to the next car. When I entered, I gathered my skirts up and continued to shout at the top my lungs, banging on compartment doors as I passed.

"Help! Mr. Dubois! He is the murderer!"

I reached the last car, just before the caboose, and raced past the young Mr. Farrow.

"Miss Fairweather!" he cried.

"Get help!" I shouted.

I could not stop. I had one chance. I must isolate my pursuer, trap him...

I dashed out onto the small platform at the back of the caboose, the tracks *cli-clicking* away from me. The wind whipped my hair into my eyes and made it difficult to breathe. The darkness pressed in around me from all sides.

My vision tunneled and a rim of shadow appeared in my periphery.

My stomach heaved and I had to swallow to keep the bile down.

Jerome...Jerome...

I clung to the railing desperately. It would be the only thing that would keep me from falling over the side.

Mr. Dubois appeared a moment later...just as I expected he would.

I did not have to pretend to turn to him in horror. I knew full well that this plan might very well backfire, and I would be tossed from the train before anyone was able to follow me out to rescue me. Had anyone listened to me? Had Mr. Farrow gone to get help as I had asked him to?

"You are certainly faster than you look," my enemy said, wiping his nose with the sleeve of his coat. "Why did you run all the way out here? You do realize that you would have done better to stay where people would have been able to find you? To help you?"

He pulled the door closed behind himself, and with the *thud* that finalized the movement, I wondered if it was not a great deal like the last strike on the last nail in my own coffin.

This will either be the best decision I could have made...or the very worst.

I examined my heart and realized the fear was fast fading. Tranquility came over me, stilling the worries like a ripple disappearing from a quiet pond.

If Jerome had been killed...then it hardly mattered what happened next, did it?

Either way, I had lost the person that I cared about more than any other in the world. I did not care for the other passengers, except Mrs. Montford. I did not even care a great deal about the fate of Mr. Bedeau, in that moment.

All I could see in my mind was Jerome sprawled across the floor...not moving, not even seeming to be breathing.

Perhaps gone. Gone forever.

And then what?

What would that mean for me?

"You do not frighten me," I said, staring Mr. Dubois straight in the face. "I will not cower like some church mouse before you."

He smirked, taking a slow, deliberate step toward me. He had dropped the metal bar sometime during our chase but I had no doubt he was capable of killing me without it. "Well, now..." His eyes narrowed to slits. "I assume you loved that man in there?"

My heart hitched at the question. "Yes," I said, without reservation.

He nodded. "I thought as much," he said.

He took another step toward me. I did not flinch. I simply stared at him. There was nothing he could do to me now that would harm me. He had taken the only earthly happiness I had known in many years.

"But my, you are a pretty thing," he said, a smile spreading across his face. He reached up and ran the flat of his palm across his jawline. "And rather clever, too, spotting the suitcase as you did. Perhaps I am going about this all wrong...perhaps you are, as well."

My heart quickened ever so slightly but my expression remained steely.

"What would you say to joining me?" he asked.

My eyes narrowed. "What do you mean? Join you in your – your murdering spree?"

He laughed. "Well, it seems I cannot read you well, can I?" he asked. "No, of course not. What did you think the suit-case full of money and gold was? Did you figure it out?"

I tried to swallow but my throat had grown tight. "No," I said.

His smirk curled more wickedly. "I am what you might call a bank robber."

A cold chill passed down my spine. A professional criminal?

"I am currently wanted in six different countries, with varying bounties upon my head," he said. "They have yet to catch me. I doubt they ever will."

The suitcase certainly made sense now.

"There would be a great deal of wealth in it for you, if you did join me. I could certainly use a partner like you. Somehow you managed to figure out that I was the one who killed Mr. Bedeau, and in so few hours... Of course, no one would expect someone such as yourself to be a thief, as quiet and lovely as you are, and – "

"No," I said, disgust painting every word. "Why would you ever think that I would want to help you?"

He frowned, his brow furrowing. "You did not even allow me the chance to finish my thought," he said. "What I was about to share is that I would happily split the earnings forty-sixty with you."

"I already said no," I said through my clenched teeth.

He shrugged. "It is a handsome offer, you know. My first offer was to be thirty-five-sixty-five, but I suppose you would not know that, as unfamiliar with the business as – "

"I am not a thief!" I shouted. "And I will not join you!"

Mr. Dubois's expression went from playful to suddenly quite hardened. "That was your only chance," he said, his voice so low it might have passed as a growl. "You had two ways off this train. One would be to accompany me, work alongside me, help me to further my ends. I would offer you protection, clothing, jewels...anything you would ever dream of."

He shook his head.

"But the other way off this train? Well...it will be over the side of the rails, darling. After I kill you, that is."

He started toward me when I threw up my hands.

"Why did you kill Mr. Bedeau?" I asked.

He stopped and sighed. "Really? I suppose I am not as regretful as I thought I might be, having to kill you, if you are as simple as all this. I killed Mr. Bedeau because he, too, saw the suitcase."

He shrugged his shoulders.

"It's a shame, really. If he had simply left me alone, not disturbed me when I was counting all my money..." he said.

"You killed him because he – he checked on you?" I asked. "Were you not the one who let him in?"

"I wanted to know who it was that was bothering me after midnight," Mr. Dubois said, frowning even deeper. "Unfortunately, he was rather nosey...and as such, he saw more than he should have, and then I had no choice."

"Why could you not have lied to him?" I asked. "Would

that not have been easier? Telling him that the money was from a recent inheritance or some such."

"Did you not hear me a moment ago?" he asked, his voice raising. "I am wanted in *six* countries! Why would I leave something to chance when the slightest whisper about me could reach the authorities and have me found?"

"You have evaded them this long, haven't you?" I asked. "And you seem to be oh so clever, aren't you? If you had thought of a less violent way out, we would not be having this conversation and you would not have been caught."

"Have I been caught, though?" he asked with a laugh. "My dear girl, you do not seem to realize that you have walked right out onto this platform to meet your doom."

I swallowed. Was this it? Had I come to meet my end?

I closed my eyes. This was not how Jerome would want things to end. He would want me to fight. He would want me to see this through.

"Any last words?" Mr. Dubois asked. "Though I suppose there is little point, is there? The man who would have cared to hear them is surely growing cold in that dark, empty hallway – "

I lashed out at him without thought. The anger surged to the surface like steam erupting from a boiling kettle. I jumped on him and dug at his face with my fingernails.

He screamed in pain, stumbling backward until his back slammed into the exterior door.

He tried to grab at me but I would not relent. I had drawn lines of blood across his face, and was just raising my hand to swipe my nails across his eyes when the door suddenly opened, and Mr. Dubois fell inside.

Before I had the chance to launch myself at him once again, I was hoisted up off of Mr. Dubois' scrambling figure.

"Anna – Anna, it's me!"

I froze.

Am I...am I dead already?

My feet found the ground once more and I wheeled around to see Jerome standing there, his arms firmly fixed around me as if to shield me from any further harm.

"Jerome..." I breathed.

I threw my arms around his neck and he held me tightly against him.

It was all I needed.

The whole world could have come down around me in that moment and I would not have cared.

Behind us, Mr. Farrow and Mr. Vaux wrestled Mr. Dubois to the ground, as he attempted to flee. Where he would go, I had little idea. We would not be stopping for some hours.

I laid my head against Jerome's chest and he rested his hand against the back of my head, stroking my hair.

He was safe. He was all right. He was alive.

If I had not fought, if I had allowed my enemy to overpower me...

I squeezed Jerome tightly and he responded likewise.

*That doesn't matter...*I thought. *It seems everything will be all right now.*

14

Venice might very well have been the most beautiful city that I had ever seen. Glistening water seemed to hold the very buildings aloft. Sunlight filtered down between the buildings, bouncing off the glass-like surface of the canals. Gondolas glided along, almost as frequent as the cars in the streets of London. It may as well have been an entirely different world.

The station stood at the edge of the city but the views I could see off in the distance had stolen my breath.

"I feel I must apologize..."

I looked up, my eyes falling upon Jerome who sat in the seat across from my own. Our compartment had been returned to its daytime setting, with the bunks returned to their place in the wall and the benches turned down and ready for the next passengers who would embark on the train.

Though I wondered if anyone would be riding this particular train for some time, or in particular, the very car that we rode in.

As far as I knew, Jerome and I were the only two people

in the entire car; everyone else had gathered their belongings and made their way to the day car where they planned to wait for our arrival in the station...which would not be more than a quarter of an hour from now.

The news of Mr. Dubois had spread through the train rapidly, as I had expected it would. He had been wrestled into one of the compartments at the back of the train. His arms tied with leather straps strong enough to repair parts of the engine, there was little he would be able to do to escape, even as clever as he was.

Mrs. Montford had insisted that we accompany her, as she had no desire to remain in the car where Mr. Bedeau had been murdered, but also knowing that Mr. Dubois' compartment was merely two down from our own. "I see nothing wrong with wanting to keep myself away from these matters," she had said, her eyebrows arching toward her hairline. "I have dealt with far too much death these past months. We all have. I do not want to dwell on it needlessly and longer than I must."

"I must speak with Anna, first," Jerome said. "There is something that I have meant to tell her that I cannot delay any longer."

Mrs. Montford seemed curious, but said nothing and instead gave us permission to return to the compartment on our own...which was how we had ended up here, all alone.

I stood at the window, peering out over the coming city. "Why do you feel you must apologize?" I asked. "If it is about what happened with Mr. Dubois, you did nothing wrong."

"No," he said, and he rose to come join me at the window.

He sighed. "I suppose it does have *something* to do with Mr. Dubois, in a way..." he said. "There is something that I have been meaning to tell you for some time and nothing apart from my own fear has prevented me."

My heart quickened within me, as I looked up at him. This sort of importance could mean only one of two possible conversations...

"I did not know what would be appropriate, either..." he said. "For the circumstances in our lives – well, your life in particular – have only so recently changed. To be perfectly honest, it certainly makes it easier for me to say this, as I realize that a great deal more is possible than what might have been before – "

"Jerome," I said. "What is it that you wish to tell me?"

"I love you, Anna," he said finally, with such weight, such finality that I knew it could only be the truth. "I have loved you for...well, I can hardly say since when. I have wanted to tell you but I hardly knew how."

"I – I see," I murmured, my mind racing. A part of me had suspected for some time that he felt something for me, and yet, I found myself unprepared to hear the words aloud.

"Have you spoken with your aunt about this?" I asked, stalling for time to think. I realized as soon as I said it that it was a strange response to his romantic declaration.

Luckily, he didn't seem to find it odd.

"Actually, I have," he said. "And she is not as opposed to my feelings for you as you might think. In fact, she supports the idea."

I frowned slightly. "I suppose that has a great deal to do with her knowledge of my father," I said.

"I have wondered the same, recently," he said.

"Perhaps it is her way of getting me out of my current role," I said. "I never would have imagined a means of not being a maid. Despite the inheritance I am eventually to have from your uncle, I suppose I thought I always would be in some sort of servant role. I do not know how to be anything else."

"It is as if when you were hired onto my aunt's staff, you lost all sense of yourself," Jerome said.

"Perhaps I did," I said. I looked up at him, frowning. "I cannot even be certain that I know who I am anymore."

He leaned in more closely. "I know who you are," he murmured.

A small chill passed down my spine as his words brushed against my cheeks, like the flutter of a butterfly wing just barely grazing my skin. "And who would that be?" I asked.

"You are someone who is brave and clever, capable of tracking down the most cunning of criminals. You also love the theatre, and you rather enjoy socializing, even if you remain quiet. You observe and you see more about others than most."

"But is this who I am?" I asked. "Bits and pieces of my past and personality – "

"You always take your tea with two sugars," Jerome said. "When you enter a room, you always give it a full sweep to ensure it is safe. When you are outside, and it is dark enough, your eyes are always cast upward as you look for stars."

I could only stare at him. It was as if he was speaking about someone else entirely. He saw me in a way that I did not even see myself.

"You never leave the house without a proper pair of gloves and you prefer to wear a pin in the left side of your hair." He took a step forward, his voice dropping. "Your mouth curves up ever so slightly when you speak of the books you read, as if lost in your own thoughts. You seem to laugh hardest at clever, witty jokes that are a play on words."

He laid a hand against my cheek, gazing into my eyes.

"And your eyes ignite like a fire when you see me..." he whispered. "So, Anna, I must know...do you love me as I have loved you?"

"Yes..." I breathed, the blueish green of his eyes the only thing I could see, all I could think of. "Yes, Jerome...I love you."

And then he kissed me as the sound of the train whistle blasted into the air.

THE SURREAL FEELING that hung over me as we rejoined Mrs. Montford remained with me even as we disembarked the train. It was unwavering as Jerome had me stay with Mrs. Montford while he went with Mr. Farrow to fetch the local authorities. Unchanged as they returned and dragged Mr. Dubois from the train, spitting angry, and hauled him away.

"They have asked us to accompany them," Jerome said, returning to Mrs. Montford and me.

"Go with them?" Mrs. Montford asked. "Why?"

"Anna and I were the ones who discovered Mr. Dubois' guilt," Jerome said with a slight shrug. "I suppose it is a mere formality."

"What are they going to do with him?" Mrs. Montford asked.

"I do not rightly know," Jerome said. "Perhaps I shall find out when we arrive."

Mercifully, the station for the local police was right across from the train station. With its golden stone and many windows, it stood as a beautiful landmark over the city.

It became quite clear to me that I had arrived in an

entirely different country when the hum of conversation all around became unfamiliar and rapid. Small phrases and bits of conversation were understandable; I had taught myself some Italian as a young girl. The majority, however, passed over my head entirely.

Upon entering the station, a pair of officers greeted Mrs. Montford and I.

The first officer, tall and thin, gave us a polite smile and asked us a question in Italian.

Mrs. Montford, to my surprise, answered him, also in Italian.

The officer nodded and disappeared, following after Jerome.

The other remained, this man much more average in build and height, with dark hair and honey-colored eyes. "I take it the lady...speaks English?" he asked, looking at me.

"Oh, yes, sir," I said. "Where are they taking the gentleman in the grey suit?"

"Back for questioning," he said. "Your Italian is superb, madam," he added, looking pointedly at Mrs. Montford.

"Thank you," she said. "My late husband and I learned together."

"Well, I am certain that will make your stay here in Venice much more pleasant," he said, but his smile faltered slightly. "Were you, uh...on the train when the murder was committed?"

"Yes, we were," she said. "Unfortunately."

"I am surprised the engineer continued his route," the officer said. "I might have expected him to stop when they found the body."

"Well, I for one am pleased that we continued on," Mrs. Montford said. "It allowed the perpetrator to be caught."

"Indeed, ma'am, indeed," the officer said. "Are you quite

certain that the man in custody is the one who murdered the conductor?"

"I could not be more certain," Mrs. Montford said.

"I see..." the officer said. His smile returned. "They will do what they can to resolve this, I can assure you. In the meantime, what has brought you and your family to our humble city?"

"Well..." Mrs. Montford said. She gave me a sidelong glance. "Would you want to tell him?"

My face colored. "I...Well, sir, I am looking for someone."

"Looking for someone?" the officer asked, frowning at me.

"Yes," I said. "My father."

The officer's eyes widened. "You do not know where he is?"

"To be honest, he has been missing for many years now," I said. "The last place I knew him to be was in Venice."

The officer pursed his lips and regarded me patiently. "How very interesting," he said. "Would you be willing to give me his name?"

"Yes, I would," I said. "Mr. Johnathon Fairweather."

The officer muttered something underneath his breath. "If you ladies would come with me, I shall set you in a more comfortable place. Now, I cannot promise you that I will find anything but I will look."

"Thank you," I said. "That would be – that would be more than I could ever ask for."

He led us to a small room off the main lobby, with a window that overlooked one of the many canals through the city. He sent one of the secretaries to get us something to eat.

"Well?" Mrs. Montford asked when the door had been pulled behind us. "How are you feeling?"

I sank down into one of the many chairs scattered around the room. "I...do not know," I said. "I suppose so much has happened, I have not yet fully had the chance to think through it all."

"I can understand," she said. "What of this idea of finding your father?"

"It is a long shot, isn't it?" I asked. "Now that we are here, I realize how unlikely it is that we will – "

The door to the waiting room swung inward and the officer returned.

"I have found your Mr. Fairweather," he said, holding out a small, handwritten note. "And he is currently residing in a home not so far from here."

15

I stood before a simple wooden door, painted red. It was flanked by stained-glass windows that reminded me of a church, and with a single wrought-iron lantern hanging above me in the small alcove above the front steps. The building looked old, with sun-faded stone walls, a crumbling front walk, and chipped blue paint on the flower boxes that hung in the windows.

When I thought of my father, I remembered a man in dark suits, with dark hair and formal tastes. Our home had no whimsy and I could not rightly remember a great deal of color on the walls or in the furnishings.

So to stand before such a vibrant door, with the sun-kissed, pale yellow walls and bright flower boxes...it seemed as if I really had never known who my father truly was.

"Are you all right?"

I looked up to see Jerome watching me carefully.

I could feel the blood surging through my veins. I swallowed hard. "I believe so," I said. "Though I won't rightly know until I see him, will I?"

"We are with you," said Mrs. Montford behind me. "Whatever it is that you choose to do."

I tried to give her a tight smile but could barely muster it.

I licked my lips and looked back at the door.

Anger and sorrow mingled together, along with a dabbling of regret and longing.

What would I find?

I bit down on the inside of my lip. What good was it doing me, standing there on the stoop, wondering? My journey had come to an end.

Well...almost.

I lifted my hand and hesitated for only a heartbeat before I let it fall against the ruby red of the door, one, two, three times in quick succession.

I took a step back, my heart quickening.

I had taken action I could not turn back from. It was irreversible now.

The distinct jostling of a lock sounded a moment later.

I reached out nervously and my hand found Jerome's. I squeezed onto it tightly as my eyes remained fixed upon the door.

When it opened...my heart nearly stopped.

The man that had been such a frequent feature in my dreams over the last fourteen years stepped out into the daylight.

I recognized him at once...but was surprised as I noticed the age in the lines of his face, in the grey at the roots of his hair. In truth, he had been quite young when he and my mother were married. Now he was not a great deal younger than some of Mrs. Montford's friends.

His eyes swept over the three of us, his dark brows furrowing together. It was a familiar action, one that he used any time he had a question about anything. "Good morning," he said in perfect English. His accent might have faded ever so slightly but I supposed that was not a great surprise given how long he had been out of the country. "How can I…"

His eyes fell upon me…and lit up.

The newspaper that I had not noticed in his hands tumbled to the ground, the papers splaying out all over the ground.

"No…it cannot be…" he said, his voice no greater than a whisper.

At once, all my fear and rage and sorrow were swiftly replaced with pure, pulsating joy, which coursed through my body like liquified sunshine. "Father…?" I chanced. "It's – it's – "

"Anna…" he said, and he took a step forward, his hand outstretched toward me.

I released Jerome and likewise approached.

He laid his hand gingerly against my cheek. Tears welled within his eyes, thick and shining. "Oh, my darling girl…"

I burst into tears at the same time and he opened his arms to me.

I embraced him, and spent the next quarter of an hour sobbing into his chest, allowing the last fourteen years of grief to depart from my soul.

I had hardly allowed myself to believe the possibility that he might still be alive. I knew, deep within my heart of hearts, that I would not be able to handle the realization of his death a second time. It was not until I saw him standing before me, saw the light of life in his eyes, that I had finally given in and allowed myself the chance to believe it.

"It's all right, dear," he murmured to me, his voice as

familiar as if I had heard it the day before. "You do not need to cry. I am here."

When the tears finally stopped and my breathing steadied, I stood to stretch my back that I had not known had been so sore. "I...I cannot believe that I am seeing you, standing here before me. "You...I watched you die, and – "

"You what?" he asked, concern darkening his face. "How could you have..."

"I came looking for you," I said. "I had overheard you speaking with someone that you were to meet them at the pier at the end of the street. You had been gone all day and I had heard you fighting with those men..."

A number of old memories had begun to make sense.

"They were men involved in some sort of black market dealings, weren't they?" I asked him.

His face fell. "It seems that you have already learned the truth. Why else would you be here?"

That was when he really looked at Mrs. Montford and his expression changed.

"Beatrice..." he murmured.

"Oh, Johnathon," she said, and her eyes glimmered with tears as well. The two embraced and I heard my father laugh for the first time in many, many years.

"What are – how did you – "

He glanced up and down the narrow stone street where his home sat.

"We should not speak of this here. Come in, all of you, please."

He stepped aside and waved us all in.

I stepped over the threshold and found myself in a cozy, humble dwelling. A simple foyer with few furnishings gave way to a hall with a single door on either side.

He walked straight to the back of the hall, where more

natural light poured in through windows in the opposite wall of the house.

As I approached, I could see one of the canals just out back, with another long row of homes on the opposite shore. A narrow stone bridge crossed the canal, connecting the two pieces of land.

The room itself, a small kitchen connected to a sitting room, at once seemed to be the most lived in. Stacks of books littered the floor beside the faded settee. The low table in the center of the room, made of a beautiful pale wood, was decorated with scratches and dings from years gone by. A quilt had been thrown over one of the chairs in the corner and a stack of pillows had been hurriedly stacked on one end of the settee.

"Please, sit down," he said, sweeping a pair of teacups off one of the round end tables. "I apologize for the mess. I hardly have company these days…"

Mrs. Montford took a seat in the other chair, which was not a match to the other, and Jerome and I sat down upon the settee.

I stared at the pillows, and found an open book within reach on the tired table beside me.

"I have been down here a great deal at night as of late," he said, grabbing an overturned pair of shoes and tucking them underneath the table. "Can't sleep as well anymore. I find the sound of the water to be calming."

A chill passed over me. It seemed we were different in that way. Perhaps water meant salvation to him. For me, it had meant his supposed end.

"Shall I make us some tea?" he asked, hurrying to the small kitchen on the opposite side of the room. "I apologize that the only tea I have is green."

"Green tea sounds lovely, thank you," I said.

I watched him scurry to the kitchen, snatching the tea kettle from the stove settled into the corner.

Jerome looked over at me and his eyebrows rose in question.

I gave him a nod of acknowledgement. For the moment, I was all right.

My father carried the kettle to the water pump and began to fill it. "I must admit, I am...very surprised to see you," he said. "I...did not expect..."

He looked over his shoulder at Jerome. "Beatrice, I assume this is your son?"

"Nephew," Mrs. Montford said. "The Colonel's sister's son."

My father's face brightened. "How wonderful," he said. "I did wonder...why is the Colonel not with you? I would have imagined he would have..."

The silence that answered his question caused his face to fall.

"Oh dear. I can only assume that it is not good news, then?"

"My husband died just a few months ago," Mrs. Montford said, though it was clear how much of a struggle it was to verbalize.

My father's hand released the water pump, which slowed to a stop, the water trickling to nothing more than a dribble from the spout. "My word..." he said, setting the kettle down on the edge of the basin. "How did it happen?" he asked, not even looking up.

"He was...murdered," Mrs. Montford said.

My father's eyes snapped up. "Murdered? But how?"

Mrs. Montford stood to her feet. "It is not as you think, Johnathon. It had nothing to do with your disappearance."

My father's expression made it clear he was both relieved and saddened at once.

"Beatrice, I – " he said, laying his hands on either side of the basin, staring out the window at the canal below. "I am so sorry."

"Yes, well..." she said. "There is nothing that can be done about it now."

He abandoned the kettle and walked over to us. "Is this your reason for coming to find me?" he asked, his brow furrowing.

"No," Mrs. Montford said. "Anna wanted to see you."

My father shifted his gaze over to me, and his face became quite sad. "How did you even learn that I was still alive?"

I shifted uncomfortably in my seat, looking down at my hands clasped tightly together in my lap. "I...remembered what happened that night."

His brow furrowed. "You were so young," he said. "Did you only just recently remember?"

"Yes," I said. "For all of my life, I thought you were dead. I have lived every day with that pain of seeing you murdered in the river the way you were."

My father's expression hardened. "I never intended for you to witness that," he said. "I am sorry, my dear. I trust that my sisters have explained all this to you since?"

I blinked at him. "Your...sisters?" I asked.

I looked over at Mrs. Montford. Of course he would not have known...

"Johnathon," Mrs. Montford said. "Anna was not taken in by your sisters as you had hoped."

My father's jaw fell open. "She – what?" he asked, rounding at me once more. "What happened to you, then?

Where have you been all these years? Did you and the Colonel take her in, Beatrice?"

Mrs. Montford shook her head. "We did not know what happened to her until four years ago."

My father's face paled. "What happened four years ago?"

"I turned eighteen and was too old to live in the orphanage any longer," I said.

His knees seemed to give way and he sagged against the other armchair, sinking into the folded quilt. "An orphanage...my own daughter..."

"You could not have known," Mrs. Montford said.

My father shook his head. "No, this is entirely my fault. If I had not – if I had simply done as I should – "

He looked at me, his face crumbling like an old statue.

"Anna, if I had known, I would have come back in a heartbeat."

I shook my head but found no words. It *was* his fault. "I only wish that you had not left me behind in the first place," I murmured.

"Anna, I had no choice, I – "

"I know," I said, interrupting him. "I read your letters to the Colonel. Mrs. Montford filled in the rest."

He frowned. "I never meant for you to find out," he said. "I did it all to protect you. Surely you must..." he sighed, pursing his lips. "No, there is no good reason for you to believe me. And why should you?"

He slapped his palm against his leg and shook his head.

"Anna...all these years, I thought you had been safely and happily settled with my sisters. If I had known that you were living in an orphanage, I – I – "

My heart ached when he did not finish his thought. "Would you have come back for me?" I whispered.

He looked at me, crestfallen. "I...don't know that I would have," he murmured. "It was never my intent for you to learn the truth about me. You would have been in danger, and I..."

He frowned at me.

"Saying it out loud to you...it seems so empty. So hollow," he said.

He looked over at Mrs. Montford. "How did you learn of Anna's predicament?" he asked.

"It was a bit random, if I am honest," she said. "You were mentioned by Mr. Floyd, if you remember him. It made me wonder how your daughter had fared, and when I sought your sisters out, I learned that they did not have Anna. The Colonel and I were redirected to the orphanage. To honor your wishes, we wanted to help her and ensure she did not end up destitute."

"What happened?" My father asked, his brow furrowing.

"The Colonel suggested we hire her onto our staff as my personal maid until we could figure out precisely what to do," Mrs. Montford said.

My father let out a long, heavy sigh.

"I realize how terrible this all must look," Mrs. Montford said, looking back and forth between him and I. "We knew that you wanted Anna to always believe you dead, and yet we did not know how to approach her without telling her the full truth." She shook her head. "Every story we thought of felt like a lie and so we thought it best to simply circumnavigate around the truth and offer her a place in our home in an ambiguous role. I debated time and again about whether I would tell her. When the Colonel died, it became a great temptation to reveal all I knew. We...ran into some difficulties that took greater priority but she slowly seemed to run into situations and people and items within our home in London that...drew memories to the surface of her mind. She found the jacket that the Colonel wore the night he pretended to kill you. After that, it all came back."

My father looked over at me. "All these years I thought your life was one of comfort and joy. I imagined you growing up alongside your cousins, learning with them, and your aunts watching over you. I trusted them. How could they have done this to me?"

"It is entirely possible that they were frightened as well," Mrs. Montford said. "They realized the danger. It seems the safety of their own children may have driven them to reject your wishes. Perhaps they never anticipated your death by murder when they had agreed to your stipulations."

"Nevertheless..." he said. "If I cannot count on my own family, then who can I rely on?"

"Mrs. Montford and the Colonel," I said, looking up at him. "They were as good as family to me these past four years."

Mrs. Montford's face paled and she simply stared at me.

"Well..." he said, looking down at his hands. "I hardly know what to say. All I can say for certain is that I missed you every single day, Anna. I thought of you every time a young girl would skip past me, or a young woman with the same blonde hair as you would pass by me. I wondered who you might have grown to be but I never thought we would get the chance to meet again."

My throat grew tight. "I never did, either."

"I hope you can find it in you to forgive me someday," he said. "I cannot begin to apologize enough for my actions, for my choices."

I sniffed and a pale blue handkerchief appeared in my sight from Jerome. I took it and held onto it tightly. "I have already forgiven you," I said. "But nothing can change the past. Or make up the time we have already lost. All we can do is move forward."

"You are right," he said. "Though I must admit, this is all a great deal to take in."

"It certainly is," I said.

He looked up and met my eye, and for a moment, we simply stared at one another.

"I do not know what moving forward will look like," I said. "It seems that we have both begun our own lives but that does not mean that we cannot reconnect in some way, does it?"

"Of course we will," he said, furrowing his brow, clearing his throat. "I would like nothing more. We have a great deal of time to make up for. I would like to know who it is that my daughter has become."

I smiled at him. The ache in my heart had changed, shifting from the scarred wounds of a young girl who had lost her father to the overwhelming lump in my throat as we both realized the many years that we had lost together.

Deep in my heart, I wanted to blame him. Perhaps I even did already but it was not entirely fair, was it? He had done what he thought he must in order to protect me.

Besides, I *wanted* my father. It was better to have him and have to work through these difficult choices he made than to not have him at all.

"I imagine it would be best for me to explain everything to you," he said in a low voice. "You deserve nothing less. I will share with you the whole of it, all of the muck that I managed to get myself into. I cannot promise you will be able to stand the sight of me when I am through, but I know now, seeing you sitting here before me, I can do nothing less for you. You deserve to know it all. If you choose to leave me behind as a result, then I shall not stop you."

I swallowed hard. I wanted to run. I knew enough. Was it so necessary that I learn the full truth? Must I understand every part of it?

"And if you would be able to find the ability within yourself, I should like to hear about your life, as well. I should like to hear the good you have known and the bad. It is a punishment that I deserve, to hear the ways that my choices affected you."

"Father," I said. "You do not deserve punishment."

"I most certainly do," he said. "And as such, I shall endure it all and ask that you leave nothing out."

I stared at him.

Perhaps we would not be able to turn back the clock and live our life the way we should have but we could try to salvage what we could, share it with one another even after the fact...and move forward.

Move forward.

"I have learned a great deal lately about leaving the past in the past," I said. "And realizing that what has happened to me has only shaped me into the person I have become. It might sound rather tired, to say it as such, but I know that I would not be who I am without the experiences that I have endured. I have had people brought into my life that I might not have known otherwise, and can now see that this life has played out as it was meant to. I have been able to help a great many people. As difficult as much of it has been, I do not think I would trade what it has done for me. The terrible things that happened to me...good came from them all."

I looked at Jerome.

"You need not fear too much for me, Father," I said. I reached over and took Jerome's hand in my own. "Life has not been as terrible for me as you might imagine. Your influence continued to permeate my life even when you were not there to raise me yourself. Mrs. Montford has been protective, as was the Colonel. In a way, I always knew that there was something different about me and the way they treated me. If it had not been for your trust in them, for your friendship, I might not have had the chance to meet the love of my life."

Jerome's face softened and he gently tightened his grip on my hand.

My father rose to his feet. "Well, at least I can have comfort that you will not be alone," he said. "Your mother... would have been very pleased to know that you have grown up as well as you have."

He looked around at Mrs. Montford.

"How long are you planning to stay?" he asked, his eyes inadvertently shifting back to me.

"As long as you would have us," I said.

He smiled. "Good...I had hoped you would say that."

16

My dearest Anna,

How delighted I was to receive your most recent letter. I have waited anxiously for the postman each morning to come around to my street, so I might ask if he had one to deliver from you. Imagine my joy when he handed me the one that sits beside me at my writing desk as we speak.

I have sent letters to many of my old friends, under a pseudonym, asking ambiguous questions so that I might assess the situation I left behind me in London. If I ever hope to return, I must ensure with utter confidence that these nightmares of my past will not ever resurrect themselves, lest I endanger not only you, but all those whom you have come to hold dear. I realize that you have made allies and enemies of your own, given the investigations that you and Jerome have conducted, but that does not mean that we can be too careful. Hatred rarely dies, unless those who have succumbed to it have also perished. As soon as I have heard anything further, I will not wait a moment to send word to you. After that, I hope that I may begin the process of returning *to London. It may be a year or more before I can be certain but I know that I want to be nearer to you than I am now. The two weeks we had here in Venice simply were not enough and I want to ensure that I am able to do what I can to make up for the time that I lost for us.*

I sighed, my heart sinking. It seemed he had not fully understood me when I told him that I had forgiven him and that I no longer blamed him for what happened. The important part was that we had been reunited. That was all that mattered from now on.

There was a knock on the door to the parlor, and I turned. "Come in," I said.

Selina's pretty face appeared, beaming, as she carried in a tray. "Good afternoon, Miss Fairweather."

I frowned at her. "Selina, how many times must I – "

"I know, I know," she said, her grin mischievous. She set the tray down on the low table in front of the sofa. She straightened and folded her hands before her, a practiced motion for her position within the household. "You asked me not to call you that."

I stared at her. She wore a simple black dress, adorned with a clean white apron. She wore a white bonnet in her auburn hair and black stockings and shoes.

Just a few weeks ago, she and I would have been one and the same, yet I stood across from her in a green dress that fell to my knees, with a pair of polished taupe shoes with a small heel.

"I will always be Anna," I said, shaking my head. "I cannot bear to have you think of me otherwise."

"You need not fear it from me, dear friend," Selina said. "Though I imagine you shall never convince George otherwise. He can hardly look you in the eye these days. The other servants, too."

I looked down. "I know," I said. "It makes me feel as if I am a stranger in the place I have called home these four years."

"You can hardly blame George," she said, not unkindly. "He does not wish to overstep his bounds. He is worried that you see him differently."

"But of course I do not," I said, pacing back and forth in front of the bay window overlooking the street in front of the house. "How could I? I have not changed."

"No, but we all know the truth now, don't we?" she asked.

I paused, looking at her. "Selina, it does not change the past four years," I said. "I served faithfully and was honored to do so."

"Yes, but that is not what you were meant to be doing," Selina said. "To some, it might feel as if you have never been as you said you were, simply because this was never the life you were meant to have."

"But it *was* the life I was meant to have," I said, my brow furrowing. "Don't you see? I am no different than any of you. I lived my entire life in an orphanage after my father died, and when Mrs. Montford hired me, I thought it to be the best opportunity I could be afforded. Security, food on the table, a beautiful home to serve in...what more could I have wanted?"

Selina nodded. "You do not need to explain this to me again, Anna. *I* understand. But you and I have always understood one another."

"And you do not see me any differently?" I asked.

Selina shrugged. "Why would I care if you are not serving alongside me any longer? You have other responsibilities in your life now that you must embrace. Just because it is not as a maid does not mean that they are any less difficult for you."

I let out a breath. "Thank you," I said.

"Not at all," she said. "I always knew there was something different about you. The way that Mrs. Montford treated you, elevated your position. Knowing the truth now, it makes sense that she wished to care for you in a special way. That is not to say that she or the Colonel were anything but fair to myself and the rest of the staff...but when we learned of the inheritance that he left you, it simply confirmed what I think many of us knew all along."

"And what was that?" I asked.

Selina's smile grew ever so slightly. "That you were not meant for this sort of life," she said simply. "Some of the staff thought that you were under some sort of special protection from the Colonel and Mrs. Montford, which was not entirely wrong, I suppose."

She shook her head. "Of course, your life will not be easy now, just because you are no longer a maid. You will face new trials that you may never have realized were possible until you spent time in that world."

"You are right, of course," I said.

Selina grinned. "But that does not mean that you will not have joy, as well. We all must choose joy, yes? And if we do...then everything else can fall into place."

"You are right," I repeated.

"Good," she said. "I also expect you to invite me for tea, on occasion. And if that handsome fiancé of yours ever has a friend who might be looking for a girl with perhaps too much attitude – "

I laughed.

A face appeared around the corner of the doorway. "Mr. Townson has arrived." It was George, and he looked at me with large, round eyes. "Miss Fairweather."

I sighed, my shoulders sagging. "George, I shall not ask you again. Please call me – "

But he was gone.

Selina smiled, shaking her head. "We will work on that," she murmured.

Jerome appeared not more than a moment later, striding through the doorway in a pale grey suit with a forest green vest and tie beneath.

My spirits soared. It was as if I were finally coming home once again.

Selina slipped out of the room, pulling the door closed behind her...but I hardly noticed.

Jerome walked over to me, and as if it were as natural as breathing, I slipped my hands into his.

"My dear..." he said, his smile growing. "How are you this fine afternoon?"

"Much better now," I said, my own smile stretching across my face. "How are preparations going?"

"It seems that everything is falling into place," he said. "Reverend Phillips is looking forward to coming over to meet you tomorrow, and I received a letter from the tailor that my suit shall be ready come Friday."

"Wonderful," I said. "I spoke with the florist this morning, and of course, your aunt has scheduled me to see her seamstress friend. I thought she might be the best choice."

"She is quite good, yes," Jerome said. "I know it will make my aunt very happy."

His gaze sharpened.

"But is all of this making *you* happy?" he asked.

"Well, of course," I said. "Why would it not?"

His smile grew. "I realize that you have spent a great deal of time tending to the happiness of other people. I hope you see that now you are free to choose to do as you please, to go where you please, and to have the exact wedding that you please."

I smiled at him. "I know that it will take some time for me to allow myself the luxury of thinking of what *I* want," I said. "But do you know what it is that I really want? The one thing that I know for certain I have chosen for myself?"

"What's that?" Jerome asked.

I reached up and took his face into my hands and kissed him ever so gently.

"You..." I whispered. "You, from the very beginning of all this. When I met you that night, you swept me off my feet. You confused me, frustrated me, and I entirely misread you after your uncle died. I thought your interest in me was purely because of the help I could provide, but as time went on...your interest never seemed to wane. The more I spent time with you, the more I wanted to be with you...but I never could allow myself to fall in love."

He smiled. "Yet it seems that you failed yourself in that regard."

"I did," I said. "It seems that my heart knew more than even what I could comprehend. It did not matter the distance between us. We shared so much, in our experiences, in the solving of the murders..."

I smirked up at him.

"Who would have thought that something so terrible would turn out so wonderful for the both of us?"

"It is one of the mysteries of life, isn't it?" Jerome asked.

"I am happy," I said. "In fact, I cannot remember a time in my life when I was happier than I am at this very moment."

As I said the words, I realized they were entirely true. I knew there could be times ahead that might not be so pleasant. We might face more trials. It was possible we might even share other dangerous adventures. But whatever happened, I knew we would be all right. Because we would be together.

Begin a new series from Blythe Baker, with "A Thread of Madness: The Dickinson Sisters Mysteries, Book 1."

ABOUT THE AUTHOR

Blythe Baker is the lead writer behind several popular historical and paranormal mystery series. When Blythe isn't buried under clues, suspects, and motives, she's acting as chauffeur to her children and head groomer to her household of beloved pets. She enjoys walking her dog, lounging in her backyard hammock, and fiddling with graphic design. She also likes binge-watching mystery shows on TV.

To learn more about Blythe, visit her website and sign up for her newsletter at

Made in the USA
Coppell, TX
03 October 2021

63428685R00100